President (
and
the 'Disappearance' of Laura Post

John Post

March 2019

To Helen,

Antoinette's esteemed colleague
+ my book buddy !! :)
Isabella and I hope you enjoy
this epistolatory novel.

John xx

i

ISBN: 9781723773686

Dedication
For Laura

Laura was never one to stand still. Even as a small child she missed out on crawling, simply standing up one day and walking across the room. It felt like she never sat down again.

What follows are the letters she sent over a two year period to President Grump, starting in February 2016, when Murica and the rest of the world still viewed him as a long shot candidate for the Murican Presidency.

In her writing, Laura found that she unintentionally influenced David Grump when he began to take her ideas and make them his own. As she continued sending her letters, her reasons for writing changed. With a new purpose, she discovered her ability to influence other people, quite apart from the President. And she discovered that her influence grew beyond anything she could ever have imagined.

Her letters were first published in late January 2018 by the Heligan Times. But, like Laura, her story has not stood still. This publication pairs her letters with David Grump's texts to Laura, some of his many tweets, as well as news items of the time.

The book is dedicated to my daughter Laura and her generation, who make the world a better place.

John Post
Allegiant City   March 2019

1

2535 Rustican Road
Allegiant City
Suruina 95411

Mr David Grump
2713 Hiassen Drive
Thawle
Heligan 62226

February 10th 2016

Dear Mr Grump

I am writing to you because my dad's happy. He's happy for the first time in a long time and I wanted to thank you.

My name is Laura Post and I am 12 years old. I live with my mom and dad and younger brother Clint in the house where I was born. It's about half way up a sloping street. Go outside and you can see the pithead at the bottom of the hill. At the top is the church, where we go each Sunday to pray. The small tree outside my bedroom window is bare. As I look out, I hear the constant hum of the mine and the horn announcing the end of another shift. I see a few trucks driving by and people lining up outside the dollar store.

My mom says we are lucky. "Laura," she says, "although we live on the wrong side of the tracks, we have a roof over our heads and food on the table at the end of each day. Your father has a job and we keep warm in winter." The tracks she is talking about are the train tracks that cut our town in half, and which take the coking coal from my Dad's mine down to Newport and the waiting ships that then take the coal half way around the world to Ndroga.

Mom may say we are lucky, but I don't always feel it when I see my dad looking sad. He always tries to stay positive for us, but his smile doesn't make it to his eyes. I see how sad he really is and don't know what to do.

But that's all changed since you've been running for President. So, thank you. It's

3

the first time I have seen my dad really smile in ages. There is laughter in our house again. I asked him why he likes you. He said, "Grump stands for the working man. He's going to bring jobs back to Murica."

Anyway, I gotta go. Thank you for looking out for people like us, for listening to us and hearing what we have to say.

Sincerely

Laura Post

PS The snow is beginning to melt. I think Spring is around the corner – yay global warming!

Feb. 15, 2016

Another rambling crowd pleaser

Ever since deciding to run for President over six months ago, David Grump's campaign has lacked direction or any coherent message. Today's rambling speech at a rally in his home town of Thawle was no exception. Candidate Grump talked about rally numbers, phones, the press, Muslim shooters, guns, heroin, education, border protection, and the people of Murica. Those attending the rally cheered him on.

"We have a movement going, something very special. Look at those people back there. Hello press. Hello press. We love the press."

"We have been packed. They're talking about it all over the world. This movement. It's the greatest story you've ever seen. We have packed every single venue - thousands. We had numbers no one else has ever had. And we are going to keep it going. I wanna thank you."

"So this all began on June 16th. Who knew it was going to happen. I've won a lot in my life. I've won some club championships. But if I win this, I'm not going to be playing much golf. It takes a lot to win a club championship. Running for President takes guts. I didn't know this was going to happen."

"And the people of Suruina were absolutely fantastic. You know what their biggest problem was? You're going to educate your children with love and locally. We are going to protect our right to carry guns. If we had guns on the other side in so many different shootings there would not be so many dead. If we had that.... I tell you what, if guns were pointed in the opposite direction. That shooting, where 14 were shot recently. 14 right? She probably radicalized him. They were radicalized, who cares. Radicalized Islamic terrorists. So, we are going to protest our right to carry guns."

"Big story, boycott the phone makers. Give me a break they don't want to open up the phones. We have to be smart. See where the threats are coming from. The government owns the phones. Boycott them until they do it. Who cares? We have to be smart. We have to be vigilant. So many enemies out there."

"But what was their big problem? So I go in. Their big problem? Heroin. Drugs. The most beautiful area. The most beautiful place. The greatest people. These people are great. Every place they're great. You are great. They're great. No matter where we go, the people of this country are unbelievable. The potential of the people in our country... unbelievable."

"Now, remember this, in Suruina they said to me, "Mr Grump it's heroin. The drugs are pouring in." You would never think. You can't even associate it. We're going to close up that border and I owe them. I owe them. No matter where I went what they really talked about is the tremendous drug explosion. And it just seems so strange because you look at it. It's so beautiful with the trees and everything. And every meeting I went to they talked about heroin, heroin, heroin and its pouring in. And I said to 'em, you know what? I'm going to close up that border. I'm going to close up.... I'm going to close up that border. And it will be beautiful. It has to be beautiful because some day they will probably name it after Grump. I have to make sure it's beautiful. Right?"

"And I owe it to them. I owe it to them. We've got to seal it up. We've got to stop it. And I made the promise to them and it's a promise to the country. That's a promise to the country. That's a promise to the country. Some places don't have it so bad, but it's a promise to the country."

"We're going to close up that border. We're going to let our border patrol people.... they're a phenomenal people. We're going to work with them. Let 'em do their job. They called me. I didn't call them. They said to me, "Mr Grump, please come, please come. We want to do our jobs." They're told to stand back. People walk right in front of them. Beautiful people, they've got the guns, the weapons and they want to do it. They are told to stand back. People drive through the border loaded up with drugs. We get the drugs, they get the cash. They drive back."

"We're going to run our country properly. I know the game better than any human being that's ever lived. Nobody knows it better. Nobody."

Grump closed his 40 minute speech by saying, "You are going to remember this evening. We're going to make you proud of your country. You are going to be so proud of your President. You are going to be so proud of your President. You are going to be so proud of your President. We're going to start winning, winning again. We're going to become the smart country. I love you folks. Thank you everybody. We love you folks."

Supporters appeared to hang on his every word, cheering their candidate as he left the podium. It remains to be seen whether the people of Murica, who Grump called so great, will also see promise in his many different messages.

David Grump trails his opponent Emily Cluster by 20 points.

2535 Rustican Road
Allegiant City
Suruina 95411

Mr David Grump
2713 Hiassen Drive
Thawle
Heligan 62226

March 8th 2016

Dear Mr Grump

I hope you are good and not having to work too hard. I thought you might like to know a bit more about one of your fans…. that's me!

I go to the Annabel Bishop School in Allegiant City, where I am in 6th Grade. At the moment, my favorite class is Social Studies with Ms Weber. Last year we learned about the Murican Revolution. We had to write a newspaper article about the victory of the Murican patriots, but you could write it from either point of view – the victorious Muricans or the losing colonial forces. Most kids in my class chose to write it from the Murican point of view. I chose to report as an eye witness member of the defeated army. It was really interesting, because it taught us that there is always more than one side to a story. Ms Weber's cool like that, getting us to question things and look at what's going on from different points of view.

This year we are learning about ancient civilizations. I love learning about different cultures and what they have to teach us today. I like listening to music from all over the world on my new phone I got for birthday and Christmas last year.

We had another dump of snow a few days ago, so my feet get cold walking to school. No sign of Spring just yet after all. I like that we get new growth in the Spring.

Thanks again for running for President. I saw you on the news talking about bringing jobs back to Murica. I guess it's all about jobs, jobs, jobs and that's a good thing. In the past, when I have listened to my dad and his buddies talking, it was always about lay-offs from the mine and how "the system's rigged," whatever that means.

Before I was born, there was a big steelworks in the town where my dad was a supervisor. Then it closed. I guess they could make the steel cheaper somewhere else. My dad and a lot of his friends lost their jobs and had to rely on welfare until he got a job at the mine. Mom said he hated the handouts. Now he's a miner, laboring at the coal face along with the men he used to supervise.

It feels like men like my dad have been forgotten, along with so many others. It's like nobody cares. Surely it doesn't have to be this way? Please keep working for us, fighting for us and help us to turn things around. My dad is a proud man and wants to stand on his own two feet. He really believes you can help him.

You are going to make Murica great again!

Sincerely

Laura Post

PS Today we learned about David and Goliath in religious studies. I get teased at school because I'm small like David. I don't care – it's a cool story. Perhaps you will be our real David, fighting all the people in Heligan, who don't really care and holding them accountable.

The Heligan Times

Mar. 24, 2016

Grump draws biggest crowd of the campaign

After what has often appeared to be a directionless and incoherent campaign to date, David Grump today seemed to find his stride. In one of the most fluent speeches of his campaign, candidate Grump drew a crowd in the tens of thousands. Many carried placards with the message, "The Silent Majority Go with Grump." Before coming to the podium, there were cries of, "Grump, Grump." Enjoying the adulation of the crowd, Grump said:

"I represent the forgotten men of Murica. I have listened to you and heard you. Many towns that were once thriving and humming are now in a state of despair. It doesn't have to be this way. We can turn things around."

"The people who rigged the system for their benefit will do anything to keep things exactly as they are. The people who rigged the system are supporting Emily Cluster, because they know that as long as she is in charge nothing will ever change. The inner cities will remain poor. The factories will remain closed. Emily Cluster and her friends want to scare the Murican people out of voting for a better future. In a Grump Presidency, the Murican worker will finally have a President who will protect them and fight for them. We will make Murica the best place in the world to start a business, hire workers and open a factory. It's all about jobs, jobs, jobs."

"I will bring Spring to Murica. And with that Spring will come new growth. Like David in the bible, I will fight the Goliath of the political elites in Heligan. I will keep working for you. I will hold them to account. Let's make Murica great again."

2535 Rustican Road
Allegiant City
Suruina 95411

Mr David Grump
2713 Hiassen Drive
Thawle
Heligan 62226

April 18th 2016

Dear Mr Grump

How are you? I have been following you on the TV and listening to some of your speeches. It's been fun.

I hope my letters may be inspiring you to make sure that working men like my dad have a place in a better Murica. My friends at school say I'm really stupid to keep writing to you. Maybe they're right. I mean, I'm not even sure if you are getting my letters. Oh well....

My mom has a question.... She says it's all very well you helping the forgotten men of Murica, but what about the forgotten women? Mom worries all the time. I know we don't have much money and I do what I can to help her around the house, but everything is very expensive. Can you help us with that? She goes out to clean houses to help our family, but then has to pay someone to watch Clint. Mom also volunteers at the local shelter, cooking for the families and talking with the other moms. She works really hard and she's always tired at night. One time I heard her crying. She was saying to my dad that because of paying for childcare and taxes, she had nothing to show for all her hard work. What was the point? My dad says that so much of what he earns is taken in tax too. And when he dies, he says he will be taxed some more.

If he's paid taxes his whole life, that's just plain wrong. When you become President, could you perhaps take a bit less from him and Mom, and take a bit more from other people who can afford it better? Thank you.

In Current Affairs at school we have been learning about the atrocities in Asria – the destruction of whole towns, bombings of women and children, chemical attacks. It's so sad. I don't understand how people can do the things they say are happening to each other. They seem so full of hate. I don't think hate can solve anything. It just creates more hate.

When we sit down for dinner, I tell Mom and my dad about my day. So I was telling them about the poor Asrians. My dad says we should bomb them all. What do you think?

Sincerely

Laura Post

PS I have dreams that Asrians will come to Murica and start murdering us.

PPS I know you must be really busy and don't have time to write back to everyone who writes to you. But if you get the chance, it would mean the world to me if you could say, 'Hi,' sometime. My cell number is 842 391 4450.

Apr. 21, 2016

A tax plan for the working man

Dubbed a tax plan for the working men and women of Murica, David Grump announced a redistributive tax plan as part of his campaign pledges today. Critics say that while the plan may be long on vision, it is pitifully short on detail.

"Tax simplification will be a major feature of my plan. For many Murican workers, their tax rate will be zero. No Murican business will pay more than 15% of their business income in taxes. My plan will reduce the cost of childcare by allowing parents to deduct the average cost of their spending from taxes. Murican workers have paid taxes their whole lives. They should not be taxed again at death. It's just plain wrong. We will repeal it."

Grump refused to answer questions about how he would pay for tax cuts. Nor did he like the suggestion from some journalists that the major beneficiaries would end up being big business and its wealthy owners. Asked if he believed in raising taxes on the wealthy, Grump said, "I do. I do. Including myself."

Presidential Candidate Grump is still resisting making his own tax returns public.

April 22nd 2016

David Grump ✅ @realDavidGrump

09:11   We'll bomb the Asrians to hell and back.

The Heligan Times

Apr. 23, 2016

Grump to ban all Asrians from entering Murica

Grump caused uproar today by saying he will ban all Asrians from entering Murica. "I want the girls and boys of Murica to be able to sleep well at night," said a combative Grump.

2535 Rustican Road
Allegiant City
Suruina 95411

Mr David Grump
2713 Hiassen Drive
Thawle
Heligan 62226

May 4th 2016

Dear Mr Grump

I know I said I was having bad dreams about the Asrians, but shouldn't we talk to them first before we bomb them? Do you really want to bomb a lot of innocent people? That doesn't feel right. Isn't that what their government is doing?

Completely separate, why are the newspapers making such a big deal about your tax returns? What do they think you are hiding? Surely, it's none of their business?

You have said that you believe rich people should pay more tax, including you. As a rich and successful man, I am sure you pay a lot of taxes. I bet you make very big, very beautiful returns! But why shouldn't you fight hard not to overpay your tax just like everybody else?   What does the government do with everyone's taxes anyway? I know that when they take your money, they pay for education, the military, public transport. But they also waste it all over the place. Tell them there's nothing to learn from your tax returns. Tell them voters aren't interested in your tax returns, because there are bigger issues we face, like the Asrian crisis, our relationship with President Pooting in Inferhan and making Murica great again.

My dad likes that you are going to simplify things when we pay our taxes and Mom is happy that you are helping with child care. But I just heard her complain that the dollar store has put up some of its prices. How can they do that? We need to shop there. I am sure they make a fortune already. It's ridiculous. They're being allowed to get away with murder. If they are allowed to raise prices, any money we save on taxes will disappear and we will be right back where we started.

Sincerely

Laura Post

PS As I haven't heard anything from you, I guess I'll stop writing now. No worries. I know you are a very busy and important man. Good luck with your campaign!

23:11

> Hi Laura. Thank you for your letters. Just call me Grump.

The Heligan Times

May 16, 2016

Grump says voters aren't interested in his tax returns

The last time information about David Grump's income tax returns was made public, it showed that he paid zero tax to the Murican government for 5 years. He had taken advantage of a specific loophole that allowed him to report negative income.

But today, Grump denounced corporations and their executives for using loopholes and fake deductions to "get away with murder." "They make a fortune and pay no tax. It's ridiculous okay?"

Yesterday, Grump told Prime Time News "I pay substantial taxes. I make very big, very beautiful returns." But he declined to provide specifics, saying that his tax rate is "none of your business." He admitted that he fights hard to pay as little tax as possible. One of the reasons he gave is because the government in Heligan "takes your money and wastes it all over the place."

Grump concluded the interview saying that voters were not interested in his tax returns. "There's nothing to learn from them. Why do you and the rest of the media choose to focus on my tax returns when there are bigger issues we face like the Asrian crisis, building a better relationship with President Pooting and the security of our country?"

After releasing her own tax returns a week ago, David Grump's opponent, Emily Cluster sent out a 60-second ad asking, "What's David Grump hiding?" At a rally yesterday, Emily Cluster said, "You've got to ask yourself: 'Why doesn't he want to release it?'"

David Grump will be the first candidate in 40 years not to release his tax returns.

A rallying cry for the far right?

What is fast becoming a signature theme for the Grump campaign, "Make Murica Great Again," was used as the rallying cry by the far right today. In a march billed to be about bringing the plight of the Murican worker to the attention of politicians, white supremacists clashed with other marchers, chanting, "Make Murica Great Again."

Mr Grump could not be reached for comment.

2535 Rustican Road
Allegiant City
Suruina 95411

Mr David Grump
2713 Hiassen Drive
Thawle
Heligan 62226

June 18th 2016

Dear Grump

Thank you for your text. So…. you read my letters!! That's so cool. Now I'm so happy ☺

I am off school for summer break. And I got straight A's this year. Yay! Mom took me for ice cream and my dad smiled. "Good girl," he said. He wants me to be able to leave Allegiant City when I'm older.

I am sorry you have to keep working.

I don't see all the news, but I was thinking more about everyone picking on you about your tax returns. Maybe you should be more open? It's just a thought. If you aren't open, other people apart from Emily Cluster are going to wonder, "What's he trying to hide?" Or else they will see what you are doing as hypocritical. Please tell me that you didn't do anything illegal with your taxes?

I just finished watching your TV debate with Emily! You looked like a lion pacing around her. She didn't know which way to look. I didn't understand a lot of what she was saying. She threw out a lot of facts and figures, as if we should all know what she was talking about. My dad said she is a patronizing b**ch – excuse him! But she did come off kind of like that. I don't like her – she's just not warm or friendly at all.

What I did like was that you didn't answer any of the hard questions from the moderator. You just pointed out when Emily had done some crooked things, like using her personal email for government secret stuff – I call her Crooked Emily! I mean how dumb was that? And all she could come back with AGAIN was whining AGAIN about why hadn't you released your tax returns.

Did you notice how the moderator didn't stop you when you interrupted Emily and talked over her? I think she must like you. But Emily certainly doesn't!

I'm also really impressed that you play by your own rules and nobody else's. And you don't seem to care what anyone else thinks.

Sincerely

Laura

PS What's the most fun you have as a star?

16:41

> As you say, I play by my own rules. Grump does not do "should." And on my taxes, trust me, whether I did anything illegal or not, the Murican people will forget about my tax returns soon enough.

16:45

> Not sure I should tell you exactly how much fun I have as a star. But believe me, I do have fun!

June 23rd 2016

Presidential Candidate Grump was caught on tape this afternoon saying, "I like to grab women by the p***y," and stated, "When you are a star, they let you do it. They'll walk up to you and they'll flip their top and they'll flip their panties."

He went on to talk about moderator Kathy Holmes after Tuesday's debate. "I moved on her and I failed. I admit it. I wanted to f**k her and I moved on her very heavily, like a bull, but I couldn't get there. Her loss."

The Heligan Times

Jun. 24, 2016

Grump calls out "Crooked Emily"

In one of his regular tweets he said, "Crooked Emily Cluster is a fraud who has put the public and country at risk by her illegal and very stupid use of e-mails. Many missing!"

June 25th 2016

David Grump ✓ @realDavidGrump

14:35   If Emily can't satisfy her husband, what makes her think she can satisfy Murica?

June 26th 2016

David Grump ✅ @realDavidGrump

14:23   I play by my own rules and nobody else's.

Sunday, June 26, 2016

01:35

> I sure showed Emily didn't I? What a loser. Like when she got in my face that I'd paid no taxes 10 years ago and I was able to respond, "That makes me smart." By the way, I didn't understand half of what she was talking about either. It doesn't matter. Few people will vote for her anyway because of her face! LOL.

2535 Rustican Road
Allegiant City
Suruina 95411

Mr David Grump
2713 Hiassen Drive
Thawle
Heligan 62226

July 14th 2016

Dear Grump

Thank you for texting me again! I showed your text to some of my friends – the ones who told me I was stupid to write to you. They said it was fake. They just wouldn't believe it was real.

My dad said that you got caught saying some stuff about that TV moderator, who I thought liked you. I didn't hear what it was you said. Dad said it was just man talk, like when he tells jokes with his buddies.

But please be careful. Just as much as we all think you're great, there are probably a lot of people who don't. They will try to trick you and catch you like this to show you up. The press too. They just love a scandal because it sells more newspapers. Sometimes it seems as if it doesn't even matter whether it is real news or fake news. In our local paper, there's always some gossip that gets everyone talking, "Did you hear about….?" Wasn't it awful that…..?" But it's just that, gossip, so totally fake news.

I'm not sure I know what you mean about Emily Cluster's face. She's not beautiful like your wife. But that's not her fault.

There is a girl at my school called Mavis. She's older than me, in 7th Grade, and comes to school dirty and in old hand me down clothes that don't fit her. There is always dirt under her nails and sometimes she smells a bit. Mavis is quite hairy and has a moustache. She gets teased mercilessly for it. "Maeve needs to shave," everyone shouts as she goes by. I found her in the toilet the other day alone and sobbing. Like Emily, it's not her fault that she looks like she looks. I've decided I will be her friend and have her back like you have ours.

One more thing, as a 12 year old, I guess it's OK if I don't understand everything that Emily Cluster is talking about. But isn't it your job to understand her? So it kinda does matter.

Sincerely

Laura

PS You are my inspiration :)

23:50

> Your dad's right. About the locker room talk. You know. What he said about man talk and joking. All quite innocent. You're right too. About the press. Definitely one of the groups out to get me. I blame them for a lot of the negative coverage I get.

The Heligan Times

Jul. 17, 2016

Grump faces awkward questions about women

Following his comments last month about how he likes to grab women, and after he stated that he wants to be an inspiration for all young people in Murica, David Grump faced further awkward questions about his relationships with women.

He was asked if he was worried about women coming forward at some stage in the future with allegations of sexual misconduct. Despite there being no allegations on record at this time, Grump said, "I deny any and all such allegations." Then he was asked about his mother. At the time of his first divorce, Grump's mother reportedly asked, "What sort of son have I created?" Today he was asked, "What do you think your mother would say about you now?" Grump stormed off the podium without answering.

July 17th 2016

Today, David Grump came under attack for appearing to mock a reporter from the Thawle Daily who suffers with a congenital joint condition which limits the movement of his arms. The Thawle Daily said it was outraged that anyone, let alone a Presidential candidate, would criticize the physical appearance of one of its reporters.

Grump said, "I was merely mimicking what I thought would be a flustered reporter trying to get out of a statement he made long ago."

July 18th 2016

David Grump ✅ @realDavidGrump

10:03   I have tremendous respect for people who are physically challenged.

July 18th 2016

 While the story of his apparent mockery of a disabled journalist seems to have taken his behavior to a new low, Candidate Grump hit out at the media, saying they were unprofessional and intent on persecuting him. He cited Prime Time News and the Thawle Daily as left leaning, horrendously inaccurate reporters, who published error after error in what he termed, "a campaign of fake news to discredit me."

"If the disgusting and corrupt media covered me honestly and didn't put false meaning into the words I say, I would be beating Emily in the polls by 20%," Grump said on Sunday in one of seven anti-media tweets. His focus was exclusively on the news media that he says are biased in favor of Emily Cluster. "The media are flat out protecting Crooked Emily."

He also tweeted, "It is not 'freedom of the press' when newspapers and others are allowed to say and write whatever they want even if it is completely false! Fake news, fake news, fake news."

The comment was widely derided by journalists.

2535 Rustican Road
Allegiant City
Suruina 95411

Mr David Grump
2713 Hiassen Drive
Thawle
Heligan 62226

August 23rd 2016

Dear Grump

Thank you for your text. It's funny. People still don't believe that you text me, (although Mom and my dad do). Any chance you could somehow show it's you? Take a selfie? I expect they'll come around. If you tell the truth, people end up believing you.

Of course the opposite is true too. Tell a lie and eventually you get found out. We once had to write an essay at school about the story of the little boy who cried "Wolf!" You remember how he was looking after the sheep and got bored. So he cried out, "Wolf, wolf!" All the village people came running, only to find him laughing at them. A while later he did it again, "Wolf, wolf!" And again, the villagers came running. But when a wolf really did come by and the boy cried out "Wolf!" the villagers ignored him, because of his lies and the wolf got to eat the sheep. So I wrote that if you tell lies, people end up not believing you when you tell the truth. And I added that if you tell a lie, you often have to tell more lies to cover up the first one. "In the end, it'll come back and bite you in the ass," as my dad likes to say. I think the story would have been better if the little boy had gotten eaten not the sheep. But I guess it is always the poor sheep who get 'eaten' in stories and in real life.

Thankfully, you tell the truth, which is why people believe in you and why you will beat Emily Cluster.

We are all back at school now. Ugh! 7th Grade, so only 6 more years to go! We got to listen to a cool band at school yesterday – Bad Hombres. They played rock and punk music mainly and some pop. The best part came when they blew all the lights in the school. That's when the deputy principal said, "We have some bad Bad Hombres here. You better get out and go back home." He was laughing. It was so funny. He's cool our deputy principal.

So, it was Social Studies again today. We were talking about immigration and how Murica was built on immigrants coming to the country. I didn't realize that if you go back just a couple of generations, nearly everyone in our country was a first or second generation immigrant. Some were escaping persecution and abuse of different kinds, some were escaping poverty. All were in search of a better life. And Murica opened its doors in welcome.

My dad says that immigrants today take away jobs from people like him. They compete for housing and health services. I wasn't sure what he meant by competing for housing. There are plenty of houses that are empty in Allegiant. But I do see that if there were a lot more people coming to live in our town, it might make it harder for the people who grew up here to get jobs. I just feel sorry for people who want to have a better life and can't get that life in their own countries. After all, that's what my grandfather did. He came to Murica when he was a boy, escaping war in his country.

I guess it's a very complicated and very difficult subject. But could we find some of the bad ones, you know the drug dealers, the drug lords and get them out? That would allow us to let some other people in. And I think you'd better take the criminals a great distance away. If you drop them right across, they'd come back.

Sincerely

Laura

PS Do you ever have time to watch TV? I've been watching a series about ancient times in Ndroga. They built a wall 3000 miles long to keep all the invaders from the north out.

PPS I've been wondering for a while, is it my imagination or are you using some of the things I write to you about like, 'Make Murica Great Again,' 'making very big, very beautiful tax returns,' and 'fake news'?

12:35

> Immigration is a tough one. Our invaders are coming from the south. And we certainly have some bad hombres that we gotta to get out.

August 27ᵗʰ 2016

Grump vows to rid Murica of 'bad hombres'

At a press conference today, Candidate Grump said, "One of my first acts as President will be to get all of the drug lords in Murica, all of the bad ones and get them out. We have some bad hombres here and we've got to get them out."

He was not amused when someone asked him about all the good drug lords.

August 28ᵗʰ 2016

Grump calls for the building of a border wall and the removal of all illegal immigrants.

Today, on a very complicated and very difficult subject, you will get the truth. The fundamental problem with the immigration system in our country is that it serves the needs of wealthy donors, political activists and powerful, powerful politicians."

"The truth is our immigration system is worse than anybody ever realized. But the facts aren't known because the media won't report on them. The politicians won't talk about them and the special interests spend a lot of money trying to cover them up, because they are making an absolute fortune. That's the way it is."

"Number 1. In a Grump administration we're going to go about creating a new relationship between Murica and our southern neighbor, but it's going to be a fair relationship. We want fairness."

"We will build a great wall along the southern border. And our neighbor will pay for the wall. One hundred percent. They don't know it yet, but they're going to pay for it. And they're great people and great leaders but they're going to pay for the wall. On day one, we will begin working on an intangible, physical, tall, powerful, beautiful, southern border wall."

"Number 2: Anyone who illegally crosses the border will be detained until they are removed out of our country and back to the country from which they came. And they'll be brought great distances. We're not dropping them right across. Drop them across, right across, and they'd come back. We will take them great distances."

"Number 3: This is one, I think it's so great. It's hard to believe, people don't even talk about it. Zero tolerance for criminal aliens. Zero. Zero. They don't come in here."

"According to federal data, there are at least 2 million, 2 million, think of it, criminal aliens now inside of our country. 2 million people – criminal aliens. We will begin moving them out day one. As soon as I take office. Day one."

"Number 4: Block funding for sanctuary cities. We block the funding. No more funds. We will end the sanctuary cities that have resulted in so many needless deaths. That's number 4."

"Next, number 6: We are going to suspend the issuance of visas to any place where adequate screening cannot occur."

"Thank you. We're very proud of our country. Aren't we? Really?"

"Because I am proudly not a politician, because I am not beholden to any special interest, I've spent a lot of money on my campaign, I'll tell you. I write those checks. Nobody owns Grump."

"I will get this done for you and for your family. We'll do it right. You'll be proud of our country again. We'll do it right. We will accomplish all of the steps outlined above. And, when we do, peace and law and justice and prosperity will prevail. Crime will go down. Border crossings will plummet. Gangs will disappear."

2535 Rustican Road
Allegiant City
Suruina 95411

Mr David Grump
2713 Hiassen Drive
Thawle
Heligan 62226

September 14th 2016

Dear Grump

Thanks for texting. I look forward to them.

We've just started doing analysis and critical thinking in English. OK, so we were looking at your immigration speech in class..... We're both agreed it's a difficult and complicated subject, but some of what you said just didn't make sense.

I like that you started by saying it's complicated and that you are going to tell people the truth. Then you say the "system is worse than anybody ever realized. But the facts aren't known." How do we know it's worse than we realized if the facts aren't known? See what I mean? It doesn't make sense.

Also seems good to me that you want to build a new and fair relationship with our neighbor. Fairness is always good. But right afterwards, you say our neighbor is going to pay for the great border wall. How's that fair? And to say to everyone that our neighbor doesn't know this yet. Isn't that going to just annoy them?

Minor point, I think you meant to say a "tangible border wall." "Intangible" means 'unable to be touched,' 'not having a physical presence.' That wouldn't really work as a way of keeping people out.

Number 3 was a bit confusing, because you said, "This is 1," and then said "zero" several times. Overall, you had a lot of unnecessary repetition. And often you just don't speak correctly in full sentences e.g. "Number 3: This is one, I think it's so great. It's hard to believe...."

Number 4: Sorry to be a pain, but my English teacher always tells us to look words up in the dictionary if we don't understand them. 'Sanctuary,' means, 'refuge or safety from pursuit, persecution or other danger.' Our sanctuary cities may not be perfect. Unfortunately, there are always murders and other crimes taking place wherever you are. But are there more murders in sanctuary cities than regular cities?

Number 5. You skipped this number completely.

Your ending... "We're proud of our country." That was nice. But then you talk about yourself being proud not to be a politician. How is that relevant? It's not! "What's that gotta do with the price of eggs?" as Mom would say. And then at the end, you say, "You'll be proud again." But you just told people they were already proud. I don't get it.

One last thing. Gangs won't just disappear. They are always going to be around. There are gangs in Allegiant. There are gangs in our school.

Sorry if that sounds like I'm picking on you too much. I just feel lucky I get to 'talk' with you about my thoughts. I think people really like that you come at issues from a common-sense point of view. My dad certainly does. But you still actually have to make sense. So, it makes sense to arrest illegal immigrants who are criminals.

But my English teacher says that everyone in our country, whoever they are, deserves the protection of our laws. I'll have to look that up too.

Anyway, I got an A for my piece on your speech.

After we got our papers back, we were talking in class. A friend of mine, Joe, said, "Grump knows that people south of the border have ladders right?" Meaning that they could climb over. We all laughed.

Sincerely

Laura

PS And you are copying some of the things I say. I like that. I have added you to my prayers at night. God bless you and God bless me!

01:42

First, immigration is no laughing matter. But I <u>am</u> asking how high we have to make the wall so that ladders can't be used. Second, WOW! Glad your feedback wasn't directed at me. You're certainly a smart girl with a sharp tongue in your head. I just fired my speechwriter. I told him, "You're fired." I'm surrounded by incompetents and incompetence. Maybe I should hire you?

September 20ᵗʰ 2016

After a shooting in the state of Suruina by a Muslim with ties to Asria, Grump repeated his desire to bomb the Asrians to hell and back. He went on to say, "Over the last 5 years, we've admitted nearly 100,000 Asrians to our country. These people believe that the barbaric practice of honor killings against women is often or sometimes justified. That's what they say. That's what they say. They are justified."

Grump called for "a total and complete shutdown of Muslims entering Murica, until our country's representatives can figure out what is going on."

He then started to rant. There is no other way to describe Grump's behavior.

First, he equated immigration with crime. "All the people coming across our southern border, they're bringing drugs, they're bringing crime. They're rapists."

Second, he put down the people from the recently devastated island of Hiita, saying, "Everyone coming from Hiita, they all have AIDS."

He concluded with negative comments about Ewagia. "If we let them in, they will never go back to their huts."

In an angry question and answer session with the press, Grump refused to answer where he got his information from. He would not allow a comparison to be made between the number of honor killings in Murica and overall rates of domestic violence and murder, simply repeating, "Honor killings are a barbaric practice." Nor would he be drawn about what he would do to reduce rates of domestic abuse.

Indeed, appearing to downplay the importance of domestic violence against women in Murica, Grump said, "We're not here to talk about domestic violence, we are here to talk about something significant. It's an issue that is facing Murica and its people today – immigration."

We are already seeing how his ideology is likely to impact policy.

He ended the session with a somewhat odd blessing, "God bless you. God bless me. And God bless Murica."

————

For the record:

In the last 5 years, immigration statistics reveal that Murica has allowed 24,600 Asrians into the country. All were fleeing ethnic cleansing and chemical attacks by the Asrian government.

Statistics from the World Nations Organization suggest there were 5000 honor killings of women worldwide in 2000. Research quoted by the Murican Department of Justice suggest that in 2014 there were 25-27 honor killings in our country. This compares with information from the Murican Psychological Association, who state that on average, three or more women are murdered by their boyfriends or husbands each day in Murica. This equates to 1095 deaths per year. Guns are used in over half of these murders.

As Grump walked off the podium, he was heard to say, "I don't know why we want all these people from shithole countries coming here anyway."

Later, while not denying the 'shithole' remark, a Grump spokesperson said in a statement, "Grump is fighting for permanent solutions that make our country stronger by welcoming those who can contribute to our society, grow our economy and assimilate into our great nation."

Staffers predict that Grump's comments about immigration will resonate with his base.

Sep. 21, 2016

Not a racist!

In an interview with journalist Raj Mehta, when challenged about his recent comments about immigrants, Grump maintained, "No, no, I'm not a racist. I am the least racist person you have ever interviewed, that I can tell you."

September 21st 2016

David Grump ✅ @realDavidGrump

23:36   I never said anything derogatory about Hiitians other than Hiita is, obviously, a very poor and troubled country. Never said "take them out." Made up. I have a wonderful relationship with Hiitans. Probably should record future meetings - unfortunately, no trust!

2535 Rustican Road
Allegiant City
Suruina 95411

Mr David Grump
2713 Hiassen Drive
Thawle
Heligan 62226

October 24th 2016

Dear Grump

Thanks again for texting. You made me laugh, asking me to be your speech
writer! Now my friends really won't believe me!! I showed your text to my friend
Joe and he laughed too.

My dad and his buddies really liked what you said about the Asrians and
immigrants. I thought you'd like to know. As I was at school, I wasn't able to hear
exactly what you said. But I did hear you got caught by the press again saying
something about 'shithole countries.' That's a bummer. It feels like the media
just want to knock you down.

Didn't you now that your microphone was still on? It's like you have two
opponents, Emily and the media. I'm sorry. Haters gonna hate.

It reminds me of the time when my dad got caught…. He was driving in his truck
with some of his friends from work and they were going to go drinking. So, he
calls Mom on his cellphone and puts her on speaker. He says, "Hey honey, I just
drew an extra shift at the pit. Won't be home 'til later. OK babe?" He hangs up
and says to his buddies, "That's how you manage the little woman boys! That's
how you manage women. So, where's anyone want to go for that drink?" Then
he hears Mom's voice over the speaker, "You might want to hang up the phone
you ass." My dad hadn't ended the call properly. She was so mad at him. I heard
the whole thing – it was funny. My dad came straight home. Later, Mom said to
me, "Laura. And that's how you handle men!"

You just need to be more careful about what you say. If you put bad images into people's minds about 'shithole countries,' you will most likely make Muricans prejudiced against those countries. That's not what you want is it? Lots of countries have done nothing against you have they? Just sayin'. Ms Weber says that If you keep attacking, others will defend or attack back.

So, how are you feeling now we are so close to the election? You've been getting big crowds at your rallies and your polling numbers are good. But everyone's saying it's too close to call. At school we've been having our own presidential campaign with debates and everything and you won! Losers gonna lose. You got my vote.

Sincerely

Laura

PS I have faith in you. You are with us. You are a great builder and are going to solve lots of big problems. I know you will work hard and never let us down. You are going to make Murica great again, MMGA! Nobody else can do it.

23:16

> That's exactly what happened – I got caught out by the media, who we know are out to get me with their fake news. I'm excited for the election. As you say, no one else can do what I can for our country. No one can fix infrastructure like me. No one can create jobs like me. If I win, our country will be great again. God bless me!

October 29th 2016

David Grump ✅ @realDavidGrump

11:01   We now have TWO opponents – Crooked Emily and the media. We cannot let the media get away with it. We MUST fight back.

11:09   When will all the haters and losers out there realize that having a good relationship with President Pooting of Inferhan is a good thing, not a bad thing. Only stupid people, or fools, would think that it is bad!

11:18   Emily and her crew, they're always playing politics - bad for our country. I want to solve big problems - Asria, Ketor, terrorism - and Inferhan can greatly help!

13:14   The new joke in town is that Inferhan leaked those disastrous Cluster e-mails, which should never have been written (stupid), because Pooting likes me.

October 30th 2016

David Grump ✅ @realDavidGrump

19:13   I'm attracting the biggest crowds by far and the biggest poll numbers by far.

20:12   I'm the best builder. Look at everything I've built.

20:16   I will be the greatest job-producing President in Murican history.

20:18   I will bring our jobs back to Murica and keep our companies from leaving. Nobody else can do it.

October 31st 2016

David Grump ✔@realDavidGrump

23:12   I'm with YOU! I will work hard and never let you down. Make Murica Great Again!

23:16   I'm the only one who can Make Murica Great Again.

23:19   MMGA – Make Murica Great Again.

The Heligan Times

Nov. 8, 2016

Cluster poised to win

The latest polls suggest that Emily Cluster has an 85% chance to win the election.

Tuesday, November 8, 2016

22:10

> I really don't think I'm gonna win. Crooked Emily is the most corrupt person to have run for the Presidency of Murica.

2535 Rustican Road
Allegiant City
Suruina 95411

President Elect David Grump
2713 Hiassen Drive
Thawle
Heligan 62226

November 9th 2016

Dear Mr President

CONGRATULATIONS!! OMG you did it! It feels so great to write, "Dear Mr President."

I was allowed to stay up and watch some of the early returns last night. Then, when I woke up this morning, it seemed like the whole map of Murica was red. Allegiant City certainly was.

My dad's been going around with a big smile on his face all day. Mom keeps saying, "Well, now we'll have to see what he can do." That's Mom for you. My dad and I just roll our eyes at each other. At breakfast, she caught us laughing at her. Oops! "OK you two, quit your cackling. You know I think the proof of the pudding..." "Is in the eating," my dad and I chimed in. That's one of Mom's favorite sayings. "I'm just sayin'," says Mom. But my dad and I, we don't think, we know. We know it's time for us to come together. We know you are going to be a President for all Muricans.

Sincerely

Laura

PS Thank you Mr President.

Grump's Victory on Front Pages Worldwide

"Grump Triumph Shocks the World"

"House of Horrors"

"President Grump"

"Stunning Grump Win"

"It's Grump"

November 10th 2016

The Murican political establishment is reeling today as leaders in both parties begin to come to grips with four years of President David Grump, a once-unthinkable and unimaginable scenario that has now plunged Murica, its allies and adversaries into a period of deep uncertainty about his policies and the impact of his administration.

The Heligan Times

Nov. 10, 2016

David Grump's shock victory to become President

David Grump pledged that he would be a President "for all Muricans" after being elected the 45th President of Murica, capturing crucial victories over Emily Cluster in a remarkable show of strength. The President Elect was addressing supporters at a victory party in Heligan City, the day after his rival Emily Cluster called him to concede. Following what has been a bitter and bruising campaign, he went on to say, "It's time for us to come together as one united people."

November 11th 2016

David Grump ✔@realDavidGrump

08:33   Crooked Emily Cluster is the worst and biggest loser of all time. She just can't stop. Emily, get on with your life and give it another try in 3 years!

08:36   Pooting said today about Emily Cluster: "In my opinion, it is humiliating. One must be able to lose with dignity." So true!

08:44   In addition to winning the Electoral College in a landslide, I won the popular vote if you deduct the millions of people who voted illegally.

Sunday, November 12, 2016

11:15

> Laura, you're my lucky charm! My family kept telling me they thought I'd won, but I didn't want to know until it was real, until someone had made it official.

The Heligan Times

Nov. 14, 2016

A bump from Grump

As experts debate back and forth about President Elect Grump's pro-business stance, Murican stock markets have all risen since the election.

2535 Rustican Road
Allegiant City
Suruina 95411

President Elect David Grump
2713 Hiassen Drive
Thawle
Heligan 62226

December 16th 2016

Dear Mr President

I don't know about being your lucky charm. When Mom is mad at me, she calls me a bad penny. But thank you anyway.

It's my birthday today. Yay me! Thirteen – I'm a teenager. Everyone is making a big fuss about it, (which is nice) but I don't feel any different. Mom knit me a sweater and my dad gave me $20. Clint gave me a wet kiss – he calls me Lala.

I'm writing this in my bedroom looking out at the night. It's very dark and the last of the leaves came off my tree about a month ago. The first snow is just beginning to fall. I love how it transforms the black and dirt of the pit and for a little while everything is clean, peaceful and quiet. I like going out early in the morning before anyone else is up and walking out from our house a little way. It's like I'm the only person in the world. There is nothing and no one broken, ugly or hurt. I can make my mark where ever I wish. At the same time, I am conscious that I have a responsibility to place my feet carefully and not mess up a world that is so beautiful.

As we come up to Christmas, I hope you are enjoying your beautiful world and your family as I am enjoying mine. We will go to Midnight Mass on Christmas Eve. I love singing the different carols with my family. I've been helping Mom out at the shelter after school. There always seem to be more people in need at this time of year.

A couple of weeks ago, I helped her put up the nativity at our church. It looks so beautiful when you first come in.

Sincerely

Laura

PS Merry Christmas, Happy New Year and God's blessings to you. Looking forward to incredible things in 2017.

02:02

Happy Birthday Laura. I'm sure you're a very cute 13 year old. When my daughter became a teenager, she was a handful. Then when she was 17 and doing great, I had a deal with her. She made me promise, swear to her that I would never date a girl younger than her. So as she grows older the field is getting very limited. Perhaps I should date my daughter. Only joking!

December 19th 2016

David Grump ✅ @realDavidGrump

12:12   Murican Magazine called to say that I was PROBABLY going to be named "Man of the Year," like last year, but I would have to agree to an interview and a major photo shoot. I said 'probably' is no good and took a pass. Thanks anyway!

December 22nd 2016

Prime Time News PTN.COM

President Elect David Grump has been selected as Murican Magazine's Person of the Year 2016 it was revealed today.

"To be on the cover of Murican Magazine as Person of the Year is a tremendous honor," Grump told Harvey Lever after the reveal. However, the President Elect took issue with the magazine's choice to refer to him as "President of the Divided States of Murica."

Asked about the tens of thousands of protestors across the country carrying placards saying, "Not my President," Grump said, "I didn't divide them."

"They're divided now, there's a lot of division. And we're going to put Murica back together. Throughout my life, my two greatest assets have been mental stability and being, like, really smart. Crooked Emily Cluster also played these cards very hard and, as everyone knows, went down in flames. I went from VERY successful businessman, to top T.V. Star.... to President of Murica (on my first try). I think that would qualify as not smart, but genius....and a very stable genius at that! Working together, we will begin the urgent task of rebuilding our nation and renewing the Murican dream."

December 22nd 2016

David Grump ✅ @realDavidGrump

18:37   Prime Time News so embarrassed by their 100% support of Emily Cluster, and yet her loss in a landslide, that they don't know what to do.

Saturday, December 24, 2016

17:37

> Merry Christmas and a very, very, very, very, Happy New Year to you dear Laura.

Tuesday, December 27, 2016

14:01

> Since I fired my speech writer and I seem to be surrounded by incompetents, I could use your help with some ideas for my inaugural speech.

2535 Rustican Road
Allegiant City
Suruina 95411

President David Grump
2713 Hiassen Drive
Thawle
Heligan 62226

January 2nd 2017

Dear Mr President

I am honored to be asked to advise you Mr President. I will try to be like you and say it how I see it!

I took what you asked me to do really seriously. I wrote what I would want you to say to me and my family. So here are some thoughts for your speech…. Ms Weber helped me by talking through some of the ideas.

———

- Today's ceremony is huge and very special, because we are not just switching from one president to another, we are transferring power from Heligan to you the people.

- While the politicians in Heligan have flourished, the people of our country have not. Jobs have left and factories have closed. There has been little to celebrate for struggling families across our land.

- That all changes right here, right now, because this is your moment. This is your day. The forgotten men and women of Murica will be forgotten no more.

- A nation exists to serve its people. (OK, that sentence was all Ms Weber!) Muricans want great schools for their kids, safe neighborhoods for their families and good jobs for themselves. These are just and reasonable demands. But for many, the reality is different. People are trapped by poverty in our inner cities; rusted out factories are scattered like tombstones throughout our nation; our education system is broken and failing our

49

students; violent crime, gangs and a sea of drugs are drowning our nation's potential.

- Your pain is my pain. Your dreams are my dreams. The oath of office I take today is an oath of allegiance to all Muricans. I will fight for you with every breath in my body. And I will never let you down.

- When you open your heart, there is no room for prejudice. The Bible tells us how good and pleasant it is when God's people live together in unity. We must speak our minds openly, debate our disagreements honestly. When Murica is united, Murica is unstoppable.

- Murica will start winning again. We will bring back our jobs. We will bring back our wealth. And we will bring back our dreams.

- We will seek friendship and goodwill with the nations of the world. We will not seek to impose our way of life on anyone, but rather let it shine as an example for others to follow.

- So, to all Muricans in every city near and far, small and large, from mountain to mountain, from ocean to ocean, hear these words, you will never be ignored again. Every decision on trade, on taxes, on immigration, on foreign affairs will be made to benefit Murican workers and Murican families.

- Your voice, your hopes and your dreams will define our Murican destiny. And your courage, goodness and love will guide us along the way. Together, we will make Murica strong again. We will make Murica safe. We will make Murica wealthy. We will make Murica great again.

- Thank you. God bless you. And God bless Murica.

Hope this helps. I focused on some of the things you have been talking about during the campaign that I really liked. It was fun working with Ms Weber. She said she thought I had a knack for speeches. ☺

Sincerely

Laura

PS Left out the "God bless me," because you are saying this is all about the Murican people, not about you. Your role is now to serve the people.

00:13

> No turning back now. Speech tomorrow. Your ideas good. My ideas better. You know this.

The Heligan Times

Jan. 20, 2017

Mixed reactions to President Grump's inaugural address

David Grump has been sworn in as President of Murica during a ceremony in which he made a brief and challenging speech.

The refreshing promise to transfer power to the people was soon lost in his dark and angry words which drew a picture of a country under attack by Asrian terrorists, Heligan political insiders, and foreign trade competitors. A large crowd of white people wearing "Make Murica Great Again" red caps cheered the President as he said that he would "Put Murica first."

Reactions across Murica to a speech, which initially struck notes of unity, showed the same divisions exposed during the election campaign. Those who opposed Grump during the election said they found little of comfort in his words, while his supporters hailed the speech as full of hope and marking a triumphant moment in Murican history.

Elsewhere, the world's press argued that Grump's "rambling, pugnacious, protectionist speech fell frighteningly short of the dignity and optimism required at an inauguration." No olive branch was extended to all the people who did not vote for him. There was no mention of his vanquished opponent or good wishes for former President Shrub or his wife, who are both currently hospitalized but did not endorse him. The speech, "was by turns bitter, blowhard and banal. It boiled with resentment and contempt for politics and the checks and balances of the Murican system."

Others questioned his ability to meet his pledges to the forgotten men and women of Murica. An economist from the National Reserve Bank commented that history suggests protectionist policies do not "lead to prosperity and strength." "If his economic efforts end with cutting regulations and taxes flavored with protectionism, the people of the rust belt of Murica, who elected him, will not see any benefit."

In conclusion, it was "an unsettling speech that seemed to presage the emergence of an inward-looking, isolationist Murica."

January 20th 2017

<u>David Grump</u> ✅ @realDavidGrump

19:03   Wow, television ratings just out: 31 million people watched the Inauguration, 11 million more than the very good ratings from 4 years ago!

January 20th 2017

 Official estimates put the numbers attending President Grump's inauguration as far less than his predecessor. Aerial pictures show thin crowds compared with his predecessor's first inaugural speech 8 years ago.

Reactions to the inaugural speech from people on Twitter, the President's preferred communication medium, ranged from, "Inauguration speech just a mash up of campaign slogans. Sad!" to, "It's pretty obvious Grump didn't write this speech. Didn't utter loser, clown, hater, baby, stupid, sad."

Emily Cluster would not be drawn on her reaction to the President's speech. She said, "I'm here today to honor our democracy and its enduring values. I will never stop believing in our country and its future."

In other news, all mention of LGBTQ issues and global warming have been removed from the President's official website.

January 21st 2017

<u>David Grump</u> ✅ @realDavidGrump

09:46   The failing Thawle Daily has been wrong about me from the very beginning. Said I would lose the primaries, then the general election. FAKE NEWS!

January 21st 2017

 The President attacked the media for massively underestimating numbers attending his inauguration yesterday. One network suggested only 250,000 people turned out. "It's a lie," said the President, "I looked out, the field was…. it looked like a million, million and a half people."

15.15

Appreciate you saying it how you see it – wouldn't want any other way. What with fake news, the haters and losers amongst the politicians in Heligan and the incompetents that surround me, I need someone who can be direct. Three cheers to me on my viewing figures right?

2535 Rustican Road
Allegiant City
Suruina 95411

President David Grump
The Tower
Heligan City
Heligan 64617

February 5th 2017

Dear Mr President

Thank you for your text. I will do my best to be direct. But as Mom would say,
"Be careful what you ask for!"

Don't worry about the viewing figures for your speech and how many people
turned up. What's important is that you got your message across and tried to
appeal to all the Murican people.

I liked that you were able to use some of my ideas and left in the bit about "rusted
out factories are scattered like tombstones throughout our nation," and "a sea of
drugs... drowning our nation's potential." We have been learning about similes
and metaphors at school.

But wouldn't it have been better if you hadn't come across as so angry and hadn't
been so critical of all the people you are going to have to work with? I know you
don't like the "Heligan political elite," but if you are to get anything done, if you
are going to do more than just business deals, if you are to do the great things you
want to do, you are going to have to work with at least some of these people.

From your campaign, you must have learned that to influence and inspire people,
you have to show that you are listening to them, that you understand them; you
have to tell them how working with you will be good for them. I don't think it
makes sense to keep threatening them. Won't that just make them mad? It's one
thing to go head to head with a bully, like Sam sometimes does at recess with the
school bully Bobby. But you are not Sam, and the politicians are not Bobby. You

are our President and have sworn to protect our people. The politicians should be there to support you and be part of your government.

The other day, Sam and Bobby really went head to head in a big way and were yelling at each other about something. They were both so mad, but looked kinda funny as they were all red in the face. As I walked past, I couldn't help myself. Laughing, I said, "Wow, you guys just need to stop!" Still mad, they both turned to look at me. I ran!

Later, I felt bad for laughing. You see, I found out that Sam had been standing up for Joe – Bobby and his buddies had been taking all Joe's lunch money and putting his head down the toilet just because they could.

Thank goodness that you are about all Muricans, including those that need protection.

Sincerely

Laura

PS I did an internet search on viewing figures. Here's what I found out. 30.6 million people tuned in to your inaugural speech. 37.7 million tuned in to the last President's first inauguration, compared with his second, when he got 17.2 million.

Overall, the figures suggest that you have the fifth highest viewing number. Not bad!

19:44

My press secretary is angrily insisting that I drew, "The largest audience ever to witness an inauguration, period, both in person and around the globe." No surprises there. I saw it for myself. You can't argue with that. God bless me!

19:57

BTW 'should' is right. Although I don't do 'should,' the politicians should support me. I am the President. And I have over 7 million hits on social media about Crooked Emily Cluster. But most of the politicians in Heligan are jealous of me and my success. They are haters and losers. Clowns. Take the previous President..... he had no understanding of how to create jobs or opportunity; he allowed Murica to be abused and kicked around; he had no problem lying to the Murican public; he was horrible for Christians; a terrible executive; he looked like an incompetent fool – a delusional failure; he was so inelegant and un-presidential; a racist; so stupid; he was a TOTAL incompetent; perhaps the worst president in Murican history! I am the only one who can Make Murica Great Again.

The Heligan Times

Feb. 9, 2017

Crack down on immigration

In the first weeks of his administration, President Grump is planning to use expedited removal of illegal immigrants as extensively as the law allows, saying that limits on its use had contributed to a backlog of more than half a million cases in immigration court.

Immigration advocates have vowed to challenge the change, saying this could lead to the removal of immigrants who have been living in Murica for several years without even seeing a judge.

Grump has further declared an end to the so-called 'catch and release' policy. To date, those coming across the border illegally have been allowed their freedom while waiting for their cases to be heard. In practice, many disappeared. Catch and release came about because the government had nowhere to hold immigrants. Officials have now been directed to expand detention facilities. However, it will take time to build centers big enough to hold the numbers of asylum seekers that are already in the country and continue to come across the border.

And this is just the beginning. The administration is pushing its plan for a border wall. It is also calling for a status review of Sanctuary Cities and a sweeping overhaul of the legal immigration process. If the President gets his way, immigration advocates estimate that over a million people will lose the protections currently afforded them by the law and which stop them getting deported from Murica.

Arrests have already intensified with many of those arrested having no criminal record. "Everyone who is in the country illegally is now a target," said an immigration lawyer from Thawle. "It has become very aggressive."

February 10th 2017

The clock is ticking for immigrants who came to Murica as children.

At a news conference about the status the Childhood Immigration Programs (CHIPS), President Grump said, "We are going to show great heart. We are going to deal with CHIPS with heart."

The President is expected to phase out programs which grant work permits to over 700,000 immigrants brought to the country illegally as children. The original program was set up 5 years ago by President Grump's predecessor. It allowed undocumented immigrant children who were brought to the country after 2007 to obtain a two year renewable work permit. It does not provide a path to citizenship.

Critics have long decried CHIPS, saying the programs effectively give amnesty to lawbreakers and that the programs signal that if you come to Murica illegally, there are ways for you to stay. Research has shown that the programs have increased workforce participation and reduced the number of immigrant families living in poverty. The majority of Muricans say they support helping undocumented immigrants who came to the country as children.

Separately the President has made it clear that any deal with CHIPS has to be tied to funding for building his "big and beautiful" border wall. The President has told reporters that he wants $25 billion for border wall construction. Funds currently remain blocked.

February 10th 2017

David Grump ✅ @realDavidGrump

18:04   WE WILL PROTECT OUR SOUTHERN BORDER! We will be taking strong action today.

February 12th 2017

David Grump ✅ @realDavidGrump

12:18   These big flows of people are all trying to take advantage of our CHIPS. They want in on the act!

12:24   Our southern neighbor is doing very little, if not NOTHING, to stop people from flowing into Murica. They laugh at our dumb immigration laws. They must stop the big drug and people flows, or I will stop their cash cow. NEED WALL!

12:33   Border Patrol Agents are not allowed to properly do their job at the Border because of ridiculous liberal laws like Catch & Release. Getting more dangerous. Caravans of people coming. We must go to Nuclear Option to pass tough laws NOW. NO MORE CHIPS!

February 13th 2017

No more CHIPS.

Today the President said CHIPS would end within 6 months. Administration officials said their hands were tied. They described the program as unconstitutional and something they could not successfully defend in court.

This puts the 700,000 immigrants currently protected by the programs in limbo.

Feb. 14, 2017

President David Grump announces further changes to immigration laws

Several changes to immigration laws were proposed today by the Grump administration.

1. It is being proposed that all applicants for visas and legal residency in Murica will have to submit 5 years of social media, email and telephone history with their applications.

2. The immigration department has issued a memo that could tighten employers' ability to secure high skilled visas for foreign workers.

3. The Tower is reviewing a proposal which could penalize immigrants who use certain types of government programs. The rule change would substantially expand the type of benefits that could be considered as grounds to reject any immigrants' application to extend their stay in Murica or become a citizen.

4. The President has opted not to extend work permits and protections for approximately 840 Ewagians, who have been living and working in Murica for at least 16 years and in some cases decades.

5. Even though the government has rejected his request for funds and authority to do so, the President is exploring whether he can use the military to build his long promised border wall.

6. A policy of 'zero tolerance' will come into effect from the beginning of May. Any immigrants attempting to cross the border illegally will be detained and returned to their country of origin.

The administration appears to be exploring the full limits of its powers to transform the immigration system.

A spokesman said, "What we're trying to do is make it a fair system, secure the borders, put Muricans first and reform it in a way that keeps Murica safe."

February 14th 2017

David Grump ✔️@realDavidGrump

09:30   HAPPY VALENTINE'S DAY!

09:33   Have a great heart day!

2535 Rustican Road
Allegiant City
Suruina 95411

President David Grump
The Tower
Heligan City
Heligan 64617

March 8th 2017

Dear Mr President

I'm confused.

Last month I ended my letter with the comment, "Thank goodness that you are
about all Muricans, including those that need protection." At the time, I wrote it
with the very positive feeling and sense that with you as President everyone
would have a voice, everyone would be treated fairly. And when I say 'everyone' I
mean everyone in Murica, not just its citizens. It was the same when I wrote for
your speech, "Your pain is my pain. Your dreams are my dreams. The oath of
office I take today is an oath of allegiance to all Muricans. I will fight for you with
every breath in my body. And I will never let you down." When I wrote 'all,' I
again meant everyone in Murica.

Having read a lot of what has been going on about immigration, I realize that you
meant just the citizens of Murica. You said you are "going to show great heart.
We are going to deal with CHIPS with heart." Then I ask you to find it in your
heart to deal fairly with the children who came into our country, some of them 10
years ago now and who want to make a better life for themselves, just like every
other Murican citizen.

I told you that my grandfather came to our country as a boy escaping war. What I
didn't tell you is that he had come in on forged papers. The first he knew about
this was when he was 17 and applying for his drivers' license. There was no record
of him existing. Imagine how shocked he was when he realized that he had been
living illegally in his new country for over ten years.

Fortunately, the lady behind the counter did not report him. It was only when he was 30 that he received his citizenship papers. He used his story to tell us that we must always obey the laws of Murica.

Like my grandfather all those years ago, the children who have come in illegally don't know about laws. They don't know that they are illegal. They simply do what their parents tell them. Imagine if my grandfather had been deported. I probably wouldn't have been born and wouldn't now be writing to you.

So, yes, please show great heart. You see, I'm worried that your heart is actually just set on building your border wall. Using the kids protected by CHIPS to bargain for money is risking their lives. How is it showing great heart? Apart from anything else the $25 billion cost of the wall is a lot of money. Couldn't you use it for something better like education or creating jobs?

Look, I get that you want to discourage people from coming to Murica with your zero tolerance policy. So, you want to make things tougher for them. But with a lack of detention centers, where are you going to put the families that you catch and the people you arrest. With so little room to put people, I worry that you will separate innocent kids from their parents and put them in prison too. Mom says that some of the kids are bound to be very young, like the ones she sees at her shelter. She explained to me, "When kids are at such a young and tender age, all they have known and all that they rely on is the care of their parents." So, separating kids from their parents is no answer.

This can't be the final solution. It is mean and completely inhuman. A bunch of kids will grow up traumatized and with hatred in their hearts. If you do this, you will feel the full fire and fury of the Murican people come raining down on you. Pull back while you still can.

Sincerely

Laura

PS I feel bad that I gave you the idea of building a wall to keep people out in the first place. As you've said, the country is very divided already. Won't your wall be the same and divide people further? There are certainly a lot of people who don't want your wall.

07.15

> Building the wall has always been my idea not yours. You wrote that immigration is "very complicated and very difficult." I agree. Don't feel stupid or insecure. It's not your fault you don't get it! You have to understand that many other countries that Murica is very generous to, send many of their people to our country through our WEAK IMMIGRATION POLICIES. Caravans of different folk are heading here. My I.Q. is the highest and I do get it. We must pass tough laws and build the WALL. The opposition allows open borders, drugs and crime! If we have to separate families, this will only be a temporary measure not a final solution.

07:40

> I have built so many great and complicated projects, creating tens of thousands of jobs. My wall will also create jobs.

The Heligan Times

Mar. 13, 2017

Ketor's President announces successful ballistic missile test

In what is President Grump's first big test in international relations, he lashed out at Ketor's President calling him "a madman who didn't mind starving or killing his people." "You can't have a madman out there shooting rockets all over the place. Rocket Man should have been handled a long time ago. Little Rocket Man."

March 15th 2017

In an editorial published in Ketor's national daily, Grump was called "a lunatic President whose thinking faculty is at the level of preschooler and who has the symptoms of dementia."

Mar. 17, 2017

Further nuclear tests planned by Ketor

Ketor's President Yun Kwang just stated that, "the Nuclear Button is on my desk at all times."

He went on to claim that Ketor was examining plans to launch missiles toward the Murican territory of Bam. "Action is the best option in treating the elderly dotard who, hard of hearing, is uttering only what he wants to say. I will surely and definitely tame the mentally deranged Murican dotard with fire," Yun said.

March 17th 2017

David Grump ✅ @realDavidGrump

11:05   Will someone from his depleted and food starved regime please inform him that I too have a Nuclear Button, but it is a much bigger & more powerful one than his, and my Button works!

13:18   Why would Yun Kwang insult me by calling me "old," when I would NEVER call him "short and fat?" Oh well, I try so hard to be his friend – and maybe someday that will happen!

March 19th 2017

In an exchange of taunts, which marks a serious escalation in the crisis with Ketor, its state-run media say Murican President David Grump's tweet about having a bigger nuclear button than leader Yun Kwang's is the "spasm of a lunatic." "The worst crime for which he can never be pardoned is that he dared to malignantly hurt the dignity of the supreme leadership," the editorial said. "He should know that he is just a hideous criminal sentenced to death by the people of Ketor."

In response, Grump threatened Ketor with "fire and fury like the world has never seen." "Rocket Man is on a suicide mission for himself."

14:12

> You may have seen that I've been going head to head with Little Rocket Man, Yun Kwang, this week. What a loser! Sad. Stupid. Clown. Wotcha think?

2535 Rustican Road
Allegiant City
Suruina 95411

President David Grump
The Tower
Heligan City
Heligan 64617

April 1st 2017

Dear Mr President

The President of Ketor sounds like a bully.

I was talking with Mom. With bullies, she has always taught me to ignore them to start with. She says, "You don't have to turn the other cheek, but you can just walk away." If that doesn't work, she says, "Get help from an adult." Our school teaches us to set a positive example, to speak up for safety. However, my dad says, "You have to make sure you have a bigger stick and be prepared to use it." Since I'm still really short, I tend to walk away.

So, I understand that there are things we can all do to make it less likely that we'll get bullied in the first place and make the world we live in less hostile. And I guess we have to be prepared to use physical force in self defense as a last resort. But no one says that name calling and personal insults will help the situation. I feel that it's more likely this will just annoy the bully and make them angry.

For instance, sometimes I tease Clint, holding a toy he wants just out of reach – yeah, I know it's mean, but it's kind of fun too! He's little and doesn't know that if he ignored me, I would soon get tired of teasing him. Instead he calls me a "poo poo head." Now I am mad, and I push him over and then he gets mad back. "Poo poo head. Poo poo head."

Or take poor Joe, who gets bullied by Bobby and his gang. He always gets ambushed, so can't walk away. He certainly doesn't have a bigger stick – there are 5 boys that pick on him. Sam tries to stand up for him, but he can't watch out for Joe in and out of school. I am trying to get Joe to ask for help from our teacher, but she's a bit of a bully too. And he told me he's afraid of being seen as a snitch and then getting bullied even more.

Where I live, there is truth to the saying, "Snitches end in ditches." What would happen if Joe started calling his tormentors names? They'd kill him. Seriously, I'm not kidding. They'd kill him.

So how does name calling, like my little brother Clint, help the situation with Ketor? Doesn't that just mean you are playing by Ketor's rules and playing at their level – like in math, you are reduced to the lowest common denominator?

Sincerely

Laura

PS Mr President, you are now our leader. I know people look to you to be strong and to protect them. But I think they also look up to you as an example and expect you to be Presidential.

01:19

> When someone attacks me, I always attack back….except 100x more. This has nothing to do with a tirade but rather a way of life!

April 6th 2017

Grump's 'apology' for re-tweeting anti-Muslim videos

President Grump was once again in the hot seat today after re-tweeting anti-Muslim propaganda videos originally posted by a far right political group. The deputy leader of the group responded to the President's supportive action with delight, tweeting, "God bless you Grump!"

Subsequent to the President's actions, the increase in Islamophobic comments on social media has been helping disseminate hate speech and is now seen to be fueling the growing confidence of the far right.

In an interview this morning, the President was asked whether he knew that the videos were originally posted by a far right group. Grump said, "Of course I didn't know that. I know nothing about them, and I know nothing about them today other than I read a little bit. I don't know who they are. I know nothing about them."

He went on, "If you are telling me they're horrible people, horrible, racist people, I would certainly apologize if you'd like me to do that," Grump said. "As I say often, I am the least racist person that anybody is going to meet."

He "would certainly apologize," but he actually did not.

The Heligan Times

Apr. 10, 2017

Grump blames both sides for violence in Claraville

Several hundred white nationalists, white supremacists and neo-Nazis marched through the town in a torchlight parade carrying swastika flags and chanting "Blood and soil." "You will not replace us!" and "Jews will not replace us!" The group was

71

part of a Fight for Right rally. The following day, far right groups gathered on the streets wielding clubs, shields and guns to face off against counter protesters made up of anti fascist groups, local residents and clergy. Each side yelled abuse at the other before things turned violent. Clashes and skirmishes broke out with bottles and rocks being hurled.

Police, criticized for being slow to respond, eventually disbanded rally goers and counter-protestors, but not before a young white male had driven his car into a group of pedestrians, killing a 30 year old women and injuring 19 others.

One of the organizers of the Fight for Right rally said, "This represents a turning point for the people of this country. We are determined to take our country back. We will fulfill the promise of David Grump."

Reacting to the violence, the President said, "We condemn in the strongest possible terms this egregious display of hatred, bigotry and violence.... on many sides. On many sides. It's been going on for a long time in this country."

April 12ᵗʰ 2017

 In a hostile exchange with journalists representing the world's press, the President maintained his initial position on the two days of violence in Claraville.

"I think there is blame on both sides," the President said outside the Tower in Heligan City. "What about the alt left as they came charging at the alt right? You had a group on one side that was bad. You had a group on the other side that was also very violent. Nobody wants to say that. I'll say it right now. You'd know it if you were honest reporters, which many of you are not."

In failing to single out far right groups for condemnation, the President has created a moral equivalency between such groups and civil rights protestors. Members of his own party have stated, "This is simple: we must condemn and marginalize white supremacist groups, not encourage and embolden them."

Even members of Mr. Grump's own military appeared to take offense at their commander's words. Five star General Richard Lee tweeted that there is "no place for racial hatred or extremism in our military. Our core values of Honor, Courage, and Commitment frame the way the men and women in our Murican forces live and act."

The President remains unapologetic.

06:17

> The media are out to get me. The public is learning (even more so) how dishonest the Fake News is. They totally misrepresent what I say about hate, bigotry etc. Shame!

06:22

> Now they are saying I colluded with Inferhan to get elected. At least corporate earnings are up, but of course the press doesn't report all the good things I'm doing.

06:28

> And you can't get a good burger in the Tower for love or money.

The Heligan Times

Apr. 20, 2017

Hate crimes increase for the second year running say the ISF

There was an increase in the number of hate crimes carried out in Murica last year according to data released by the Internal Security Force today. This is the second consecutive year that hate crimes have increased. There were more than 6100 hate crimes reported in 2016, up from over 5800 in 2015, with 60% of victims being targeted because of their race. Crimes against Jews, Muslims and LGBTQ people all showed increases.

The ISF's report is based on law enforcement statistics from across the nation.

2535 Rustican Road
Allegiant City
Suruina 95411

President David Grump
The Tower
Heligan City
Heligan 64617

May 10th 2017

Dear Mr President

Thank you for your texts. Don't you get tired being angry and having to attack 100 times more all the time?

OK, I may not understand everything there is to know about immigration and the human rights of immigrants, but I do know that not all the media are misrepresenting you. How can they be? You <u>did</u> send out those anti-Muslim videos. You <u>did</u> say what you said about the fault being on both sides at Claraville. By not singling out the hate groups and saying what they say and do is unacceptable, don't you encourage them? Or at the very least you give permission for others to do the same thing?

Like Bobby and his gang. They broke Joe's nose a few days ago. He's still not back at school. I went to see him at his house and he said they had been calling him "faggot," and "n****r lover." He said that they had demanded that he say, "President Grump hates gays." When he refused, two of them had held him while Bobby slammed one of the rest room cubicle doors into his face over and over. Joe was found passed out on the ground. Sam told me not to, but I told Ms Weber what had happened and she went with me to the Principal. He says there is nothing he can do unless Joe makes a formal complaint, which Joe won't.

As I went out of the Principal's office, I heard him say to Ms Weber, "You need to stick to Social Studies." Why would he say that? I think he's afraid of Bobby's dad.

Without Bobby's behavior being punished, without someone saying what he does is wrong, he will simply continue to bully Joe. I'm getting really worried about

Joe's safety. You said you were going to make Murica safe again. Doesn't that mean for everyone, including those who find it difficult to fight for themselves like Joe?

And why couldn't you apologize about the anti Muslim videos or for what you said about Claraville? We all make mistakes. At dinner last night, my dad said he thinks that as President you can't afford to admit that you are wrong – that it will make you look weak. I think it makes you look human.

At the very least, please stop blaming the media and everyone else for things that go wrong. You are the President. You made an oath to the people of Murica. They are now your responsibility. Of course everyone is going to look at everything you do and potentially they are going to be critical. That's part of your job and it is not going to change. So stop complaining all the time. That's what makes you look weak! Mr President, you are the model that people want to look up to. No one likes a whiner.

What's going on with me? We had sex-ed in school today. That was depressing too. Sex is just embarrassing to me. I even get grossed out when Mom and my dad kiss. The class was all about abstinence, nothing about using a condom or going on the pill. Bobby of course was boasting, "Girls don't want me to use a rubber anyway." Gloria, who lives on our street, just had a baby girl, who she has had to put up for adoption. Gloria's fifteen.

I may think sex is gross, but shouldn't we learn about how not to get pregnant and be taught about contraception? There are too many Glorias, who don't know how easy it is to get pregnant. And too many idiots like Bobby, who are irresponsible. Mom says it's a good thing that girls in our country have a choice if they get pregnant. She says there are lots of other countries where girls can't get an abortion.

Later in class, they told us about an STD called HPV and how it was the most common sexually transmitted disease and can cause cancer of the cervix. Bobby started to look worried and asked what was his risk of getting cervical cancer? What's even sadder is that most people didn't laugh, because they didn't know either.

Thankfully, Mom has already told me about contraceptives and how condoms can not only stop you getting pregnant, but also stop the spread of diseases like HPV. Like I said, in our class there was nothing about contraception. And there was nothing about the importance of consent and nothing for LGBTQ students.

Everything seemed to be based on fear and shame. The suggestion was that anyone who engaged in sex was 'unclean.'

Like I said…. Depressing!

Sincerely

Laura

PS And you don't hate gays right?

PPS I'm sorry. I have been whining too. I just feel so mad and sad that Gloria has to give her baby away.

15.10

> Not sure I like what you say young lady. Or your tone. You should show more respect. Your friend Gloria should have used sexual refusal skills. Kept her legs together. And not that it's any of your business, I have many fabulous friends who happen to be gay, but I am more of a traditionalist.

May 19th 2017

Abstinence education funding is to be increased. In the budget deal the President signed this month, total spending on abstinence education will be brought up to $100 million for 2018.

There is no evidence that a focus on abstinence in sex education leads to lower rates of teenage pregnancy.

The Heligan Times

May 22, 2017

Dozens of women have now accused the President of sexual harassment and abuse

Over the last few months, dozens of women have come forward to accuse the President of inappropriate sexual behavior. In his book, "Grump: Art of the Turnaround," David Grump talks about women:

"Women have one of the great acts of all time. The smart ones act very feminine and needy, but inside they are real killers. The person who came up with the expression 'the weaker sex' was either very naïve or had to be kidding. I have seen women manipulate men with just a twitch of their eye – or perhaps another body part."

And then of course there were his boasts about grabbing women on the campaign trail.

In the last month alone, three women have come forward to accuse the President of inappropriate behavior. Joan Miller a fitness expert and former centerfold filed suit on Tuesday, seeking the right to speak publicly about an alleged affair between her and Grump. Also on Tuesday, a Heligan judge ruled that a defamation suit brought by Susan Knoles, a former contestant on Grump's TV show, could move ahead. Grump has been quoted as saying, "All the women on my show flirted with me consciously or unconsciously. It's to be expected."

Earlier this month, a further suit was brought by adult actress Melody Melons, who alleges an affair just months after Grump's wife had given birth to their son.

May 23rd 2017

Grump's personal lawyer, Marty Kohn, today admitted paying $130,000 to Melody Melons from his own funds in October 2016 shortly before the election in exchange for her promise not to speak out about Grump.

Initially, Kohn had denied the payment. In a statement to the Thawle Daily two weeks ago, he called the allegations "outlandish", and said they'd been "consistently denied by all parties."

But today he announced he had in fact paid Ms Melons the money. Opposition politicians are saying that this payment is an illegal campaign contribution.

The Heligan Times

May 24, 2017

Offices of Grump's fixer and personal lawyer raided by ISF

Officers from the Internal Security Force raided the Heligan offices of Marty Kohn following a referral from Special Counsel Clarice Baker, who is investigating suspected Inferhan meddling in the 2016 election.

A source told us that documents relating to the payment to Ms Melons were seized. But the payment is only one of several issues being investigated.

Mr Kohn was unavailable for comment and has not been seen in his offices for several days.

May 24th 2017

David Grump ✅ @realDavidGrump

13:07   A woman I don't know and, to the best of my knowledge, never met, is on the FRONT PAGE of the Fake News Thawle Daily saying I kissed her (for two minutes) in the lobby of the Tower twelve years ago.

13:10   Never happened! Who would do this in a public space with live security cameras running? Another False Accusation.

18:43   Same negative stories over and over again! No wonder the People no longer trust the media, whose approval ratings are correctly at their lowest levels in history!

May 27th 2017

The President caused outrage today with calls for a ban on abortion and punishments for women.

President Grump said that he has "evolved" on the issue of abortion. In an interview with Kathy Holmes, he said he was pro-choice for years. He has now changed his position and backs a ban, saying the High Court's ruling legalizing abortion should be overturned. His staff was quick to state that he believes abortion should be legal in instances of rape, incest or when the life of the mother was at risk.

"There has to be some form of punishment," Grump told Ms Holmes, referring to women who would seek to defy the ban. He refused to comment further when Holmes pointed out that pro-choice legislation protecting women's rights to abortion has been in place for the last 45 years in Murica.

Grump reversed his position two hours later, with a statement saying that he would punish doctors who performed abortions but not the women themselves.

The Heligan Times

May 29, 2017

The side effects of zero tolerance

It has been nearly a month since President Grump's zero tolerance policy for the removal of illegal immigrants came into force. Reports are now emerging that undocumented women held in detention centers are being prevented from seeking abortions and associated medical treatment.

"The Grump administration is engaging in the most flagrant violation yet seen of the constitutional right to an abortion," warned lawyers.

May 30th 2017

David Grump ✅ @realDavidGrump

01:12   The media is so after me on women. Wow, this is a tough business. Nobody has more respect for women than David Grump.

01:45   Kathy Holmes is just another journalist who is reporting negatively about me. Angry and frustrated.

May 31st 2017

Grump admits he made payment to Marty Kohn for Melody Melons' hush money.

2535 Rustican Road
Allegiant City
Suruina 95411

President David Grump
The Tower
Heligan City
Heligan 64617

June 4th 2017

Dear Mr President

Joe got hold of my phone and saw what you wrote about having gay friends, but being more of a traditionalist. He wants to know what you mean by that.

Mr President, you said I was your lucky charm. You said you appreciated me saying it how I saw it. You said, "I need someone who can be direct." But last time, when I wrote you with lots of questions, you answered none of them.

All that said, I am really not sure where to start. Perhaps with respect.

I respect the office of the President, the position you hold. It seems to me that since you became President, everyone is expecting you to behave more like a President. More than that, they are hoping you will. Each time you act in a way that is vaguely Presidential, it's almost like you can hear a collective sigh of relief as people start to think, "At last. He's got it." But your behavior keeps letting you down, keeps letting them down. And you said you would never let us down.

I looked up what you said on the campaign trail about girls flipping their panties. You may think it's OK and call it locker room banter, but it's just plain horrible and embarrassing to women. Gloria and Maeve agree with me. Mom says if you give respect, you get it back. But disrespect invites further disrespect. Even if we are to believe half of what the press is saying about your relationships with women, you bring down the office of the President.

Mom knows I'm upset with you. She gave me a hug today and said, "Honey, remember what I said about the proof of the pudding?" My dad and his buddies are still for you. You say enough to keep them believing that you are still for them. And secretly or not so secretly, they love how you act towards foreigners, women, politicians and immigrants. The old system hasn't worked for my dad for so long, that he doesn't care what you do.

But for me, what a leader does…. matters. What a leader says…. matters. And how he says it too.

Look, I don't believe you always have to be politically correct. That's one of the reasons why the Murican people love you, why you won the election and are now sitting in the Tower. It's because you are not a scripted robot. But right now, I feel so disappointed in you. I wonder whether you are just out for yourself and no one else.

Stir things up in Heligan, yes. But please don't completely mess up your Presidency.

Sincerely

Laura

PS And how could you say that about Gloria? She is a good girl and a good friend, who was the victim of abuse by her uncle. You just lashed out without having the facts.

Thursday, June 8, 2017

12.02

OK, let's call a truce. I did say I wanted you to be direct. But I don't like people who disagree with me. One of my assistants used to really annoy me, but I found a way to get back at her. I stashed a fat picture of her in my desk and I'd take it out and make her look at how disgusting she was when she irritated me. I wish I could do the same to you when you say things I don't like. As for your friend, she has now learned that life is hard. Life has been hard for me too. No one has had a harder life than me.

The Heligan Times

Jun. 9, 2017

Grump endorses Jim Olestar for Suruina Senate race

The President threw the full weight of his support behind Jim Olestar today, ending a personal endorsement call with "Got get 'em Jim."

Olestar has recently lost the support of many of his political colleagues after the Thawle Daily reported allegations of sexual misconduct with young women dating back several years. He has refused to step down as a result of the allegations, one of which is from a woman who states that he initiated sexual contact with her when she was 14 and he was in his 30's. Olestar denies all allegations.

"I am honored to receive the support and endorsement of President David Grump," Olestar said in a statement. "President Grump knows that the future of his conservative agenda hinges on this election."

June 19th 2017

David Grump ✅ @realDavidGrump

13:14   The people of Suruina will do the right thing. Meg Smith is Pro-Abortion, weak on Crime, Military and Illegal Immigration, Bad for Gun Owners and Veterans and against the WALL. Smith is a Heligan Puppet. Jim Olestar will always vote with us. VOTE JIM OLESTAR!

The Heligan Times

Jun. 19, 2017

Meg Smith wins Suruina Senate seat

Meg Smith, a supposed under-dog, has defeated Jim Olestar for the Senate seat for Suruina after a bruising campaign that saw Jim Olestar battered by accusations of sexual abuse and child molestation.

This is an upset for President Grump on two fronts. At a national level, Smith's victory reduces Grump's majority in the Senate. On the personal front, it gives the President a bloody nose for his support of Olestar's candidacy.

June 22nd 2017

Grump aide resigns

Accused of physically and emotionally abusing two wives, Presidential aide Ray Strong was forced to resign today.

In an interview with Harvey Lever of Prime Time News, the President appeared to defend Strong, "People's lives are being shattered and destroyed by a mere allegation. Some are true and some are false. Some are old and some are new. There is no recovery for someone falsely accused - life and career are gone. Is there no such thing any longer as Due Process?"

Grump went on to stress that Strong denied the allegations, saying, "He says he's innocent, and I think you have to remember that. He said very strongly yesterday that he's innocent. So you'll have to talk to him about that. But we absolutely wish him well."

Then, in an apparent contradiction of earlier comments about 'life and career gone', the President said, "I think he has a great career ahead of him."

The President has himself been accused of sexual misconduct by at least a dozen women. He too denies all such allegations.

In a statement, the President's Chief of Staff said that the President had sacked Strong an hour after hearing about the allegations. But the Director of the

Internal Security Force says a report about Strong's spousal abuse was filed with the President shortly after his inauguration in January.

This is the latest in what is becoming a long list of high profile 'leavers' from the Grump Tower. Last week, the Minister for Foreign Affairs found out he was fired via Twitter. Two months ago, the Minister had been overheard saying that the President was "a moron." Relations have been strained ever since.

In his place, two officials known for endorsing and overseeing torture have been promoted.

June 22nd 2017

David Grump ✔ @realDavidGrump

20:23   The new Fake News narrative is that there is CHAOS in the Tower. Wrong! People will always come and go, and I want strong dialogue before making a final decision. I still have some people that I want to change (always seeking perfection). There is no Chaos, only great Energy!

The Heligan Times

Jun. 23, 2017

Another resignation from Grump's Tower

Only one day after a disgraced Ray Strong was forced to resign amidst allegations of domestic abuse, President Grump's speech writer, Lars Lognar resigned today after his ex-wife accused him of domestic abuse.

In an interview with the Thawle Daily Mrs Lognar claimed that her ex-husband had run a car over her foot, put out a cigarette on her hand and thrown her against a wall. After his resignation Lognar said, "I deny these vile and malicious allegations. I was the victim of repeated physical abuse during our marriage. This is an opportunity to highlight the grossly under reported and acknowledged issue of female on male domestic violence."

The Tower Press Secretary said at the daily briefing, "I think it's fair to say we all could have done better over the last few days in dealing with this situation."

June 26th 2017

David Grump ✅ @realDavidGrump

20:11   I am totally opposed to domestic violence of any kind. Everyone knows that. It almost wouldn't even have to be said. Family is everything to me.

The Heligan Times

Jun. 26, 2017

Migrant children separated from their parents at border

The consequences of the President's zero tolerance immigration policy are repugnant, do no service to Murica and should be stopped.

The children of illegal immigrants are being forcibly separated from their parents in horrific scenes reminiscent of concentration camps. Harassing recordings have emerged of children crying out for their parents and relations. Eye witnesses have described rooms full of crying children. With the lack of available space in detention centers, authorities stated that it was thought that children separated from their parents would be fostered. But numbers have been so large that this has proved impossible. Instead, toddlers and other children are being sent to so called 'tender age' shelters. These are in fact disused warehouses in the desert where children are being held in chain link pens.

More than 2300 children have been taken from their parents since Grump's zero tolerance policy came into force last month.

Previous administrations increased deportations of illegal immigrants yet managed to avoid separating families. David Grump seems to view the practice as a useful deterrent. His Attorney General said, "If you don't want your child separated, then don't bring them across the border illegally."

June 29th 2017

David Grump ✅ @realDavidGrump

19:37   Wow, Harvey Lever was just fired from Prime Time News for "inappropriate sexual behavior in the workplace." But when will the top executives at PTN be fired for putting out so much Fake News?

June 30th 2017

Reports in today that President Grump is still consulting with Ray Strong on trade and tariffs.

Friday, June 30, 2017

01:30

> It's been a tough couple of weeks and a tough time from Ray Strong. Women just don't understand the stress that we men shoulder every day. Look at all the stress I have had to deal with over those immigrant kids. Unbelievable!

01:38

> I have days where, if I come home, and I don't want to sound too much like a superior make chauvinist, but when I come home and dinner's not ready, I go through the roof. Women just don't get that sort of stress.

01:45

> Do you understand what I'm talking about? Probably not!

2535 Rustican Road
Allegiant City
Suruina 95411

President David Grump
The Tower
Heligan City
Heligan 64617

July 2nd 2017

Dear Mr President

I have just come from church where the sermon was about the power of love. Our priest said, "As long as we open our eyes to God's grace, and open our hearts to His love, then we can create a new world. Love is all you need." In that spirit, a truce it is!

I know you are angry at the press and I am sure you are angry at the people in the Tower who you see as letting you down. I get that you are under stress. Well duh! That goes with being President right! So yes, I do understand. But you bring a lot of stuff on yourself.

What I don't understand is how could you not have seen what would happen with separating immigrant families. The thought of putting such little kids in cages.... I mean it's hard for me to even imagine. What were you thinking? Migrants are not animals.

So, do you get how you are coming across? Being so slow to condemn domestic violence and not condemning abuse more forcefully is kind of similar to you not condemning the far right groups at Claraville. You most likely would say about Ray Strong that there are two sides. I know that. But did you read what his ex-wife said about him choking her and hitting her. As for your speech writer, he even put out a lit cigarette on his wife. I don't care how much stress they were under or you are under, it doesn't excuse abuse or even you going through the roof when your dinner's not ready.

91

If you are still not convinced that I understand the stress you are under, consider this. I see my dad under stress every day of his life. He doesn't work at a desk. He works incredibly hard in a dangerous and physically demanding job, pulling coal from deep down out of the ground. My dad is in his mid 40's and works in temperatures up to 90 degrees F, 6 days a week.

At school we learned that underground mining hazards include heat exhaustion, suffocation, gas poisoning, roof collapse, rock burst, and gas explosions. Last year alone there were 5 deaths at my dad's mine. So, you may have had a hard life and be under stress. But somehow, I think my dad's life has been harder and still is harder than yours.

And when he comes home at night, he is exhausted.

My dad is always exhausted. Often, he is angry. Sometimes his dinner may not be on the table. But he never threatens Mom or me or Clint. He may bang the table really hard because he is frustrated with me for teasing Clint. But he has never smacked me, called me a horrible name or shown me a fat picture of myself. He makes the plates and knives and forks jump, which makes us all laugh, including my dad. He tries to stay mad, but he starts to laugh with us. Then Mom tells me and Clint we can be excused and I see her take my dad's head in her arms and rock him gently, without saying a word.

And of course women have stress. It's stressful for Mom wondering whether my dad will come home safely at the end of each shift. It's stressful for her seeing my dad's frustration. It's stressful for her working so hard and feeling that she isn't getting anywhere. It's stressful for her trying to make ends meet every week.

I could keep going, but I won't.

Their love for each other is what gets Mom and Dad through each day. Neither hate nor anger drives them. They look for the good in others and make a point to be grateful for what they have. They teach me and Clint to do the same through their example.

Sincerely

Laura

PS Before you were elected, you said that you would employ "only the best people." So far, your example seems to have drawn some pretty awful people to you. You say that my friend Gloria "has now learned that life is hard." But Gloria is only 15. Her abuse started when she was 6. She should not have had to learn that life was so hard at such a young age. You are 71. So, learn from your "hard life" and the "tough time" you have had over the last few weeks and make better decisions about the people you hire.

01:35

Laura, don't remind me of my age. DO NOT do this again.

01:45

Your dad sounds like a good man. I think he's going to like the tax cuts that are coming down the pipe. We've been working hard for the Murican worker to make this happen. Murican corporations are going to be happy too. They're going to take the money they are saving and reinvest it in Murican workers. It's a win win win!

The Heligan Times

Jul. 7, 2017

Tax overhaul approved by Senate

The Murican Senate today approved the largest overhaul of the Murican tax system in more than 30 years. The President says the tax cuts for corporations, small businesses and individuals will boost economic growth. The opposition says it is designed to benefit the ultra-rich and will have to be paid for by adding to the nation's already huge deficit.

July 7th 2017

David Grump ✅ @realDavidGrump

16:19   The Murican Senate just passed the biggest in history Tax Cut and Reform Bill.

16:25   The Tax Cuts are so large and so meaningful, and yet the Fake News is working overtime to follow the lead of their defeated opposition friends, and only demean. This is truly a case where the results will speak for themselves, starting very soon. Jobs, Jobs, Jobs!

July 8th 2017

The main points to the new Tax Bill.

The tax reform enacted by President David Grump contains several incentives for Murican corporations. It cuts the federal corporate tax rate substantially, from a top rate of 35 percent to 21 percent. And, for the next 5 years, it lets companies expense the full value of investments in new plant and equipment immediately, instead of over a period of years. Corporations also benefit from being able to repatriate at favorable rates cash and other assets previously held overseas.

Theoretically, investment should rise as a result. Shareholders are hoping that companies will use their cash piles to increase share buy-back programs, thus boosting share prices. The stock market has already risen in anticipation.

Individuals primarily gain from a temporary lowering of tax rates. The child tax credit has also been doubled and there is an increase in individual deductions.

July 10th 2017

David Grump ✅ @realDavidGrump

13:21   Today, it was my great honor to sign the largest TAX CUTS and reform in the history of our country.

13:55   Thanks to the historic TAX CUTS that I signed into law, your paychecks are going way UP, your taxes are going way DOWN, and Murica is once again OPEN FOR BUSINESS!

Monday, July 10, 2017

14:22

> Mark this day Laura and mark it well. It is the day that I, David Grump, will forever go down in history as the greatest jobs producing President ever.

July 14th 2017

Critics of the new tax reform bill point to a large number of glitches around actual tax policy where there remains disagreement between the two main political parties.

The last time the Senate passed a tax bill of this nature was over 30 years ago. Legislation had taken 3 years to develop and had the support of both political parties. A leading opposition spokesperson said, "This time the process was done in a matter of months and pushed through without a single opposition vote. That's why you're seeing many more errors in this legislation than usual."

July 14th 2017

David Grump ✅ @realDavidGrump

11:05　　TAX CUTS will increase investment in the Murican economy and in Murican workers, leading to higher growth, higher wages, and more JOBS!

July 27th 2017

David Grump ✅ @realDavidGrump

23:42　　My big and very popular Tax Cut and Reform Bill has taken on an unexpected new source of "love" – that is big companies and corporations showering their workers with bonuses. This is a phenomenon that nobody even thought of, and now it is the rage.

The Heligan Times

Jul. 27, 2017

Murican stock markets respond positively to Tax Reform

Stocks have soared following the announcement of the President's new tax reform bill. Shares of companies with large overseas holdings and revenues have done particularly well, as the implications of being able to repatriate billions of dollars and what this means for those companies and the economy as a whole is being more fully assessed.

Stock markets in Murica each hit new all time highs today.

July 28ᵗʰ 2017

David Grump ✅@realDavidGrump

22:17   As long as we open our eyes to God's grace - and open our hearts to God's love - then Murica will forever be the land of the free, the home of the brave, and a light unto all nations.

Monday, July 31, 2017

12:31

The Fake News Media refuses to talk about how Big and how Strong our BASE is. They show Fake Polls just like they report Fake News. Despite only negative reporting, we are doing well. Jobs are kicking in and companies are coming back to Murica. Unnecessary regulations and high taxes are being dramatically cut, and it will only get better. MUCH MORE TO COME! MAKE MURICA GREAT AGAIN.

2535 Rustican Road
Allegiant City
Suruina 95411

President David Grump
The Tower
Heligan City
Heligan 64617

August 6th 2017

Dear Mr President

I'm happy for you that the tax bill got passed. I don't understand all the details, but my dad says although there's a lot to benefit big companies and the people who own them, there are also some good things for him and Mom and people like them. My dad says it looks like it will help him for a few years with the amount of tax he will have to pay and Mom is pleased with the child benefit increase. Thank you.

I'm glad too that you seem to have had a better month, with nobody else resigning, no more sex scandals, no international crises brewing. Perhaps it's because you've been happier and less aggressive on your tweets! Or perhaps it's just because it's summer and everyone's tired of fighting. I saw you had gone to your big summer house on the beach.

Here, school's been out for over a month now. It's been really hot. Not a breath of air and not a cloud in the sky for what seems like weeks. I think the tree outside my house may be dying – it's lost all its leaves.

There is not a lot to do in our town, so I have been helping Mom at the shelter. There are so many people there and they have so little. The other day, I took in a few toys and old clothes that were too small for me. Mom said something about the shelter running out of money. That would be awful.

I spend most afternoons hanging out with Joe and Maeve or Gloria.

Gloria's baby was called Michelle, but she's gone now. Gloria said that saying goodbye to her baby was the most difficult thing she has ever had to do. She cried for days.

Some days we go to the pond and swim, but mostly we just hang out. We talk about other kids at school, laugh at dumb videos and ride our bikes. Sometimes we dream about what we are going to do once we graduate from school and get out of Allegiant. Maeve says she wants to be a nurse. Gloria wants to teach. Joe wants to be a writer and journalist but not the fake news kind!

And I want to go to university to study economics and business.

Sincerely

Laura

PS After your recent success, I have the feeling you're gonna do something or say something you will regret. I am asking you not to let this one success go to your head. You asked me to be direct. OK, then remember and be aware of how you can come across.

09:30

First, it's my tax bill. Second, your mom and dad should be grateful. I've worked really hard for this. Third, why do you hang out with losers? Are you stupid, or just a born loser too? You guys will never do anything with your lives. Fourth, don't tell me how I should be. Never forget fighting is what I do and, as with so many other things, I do it the best.

09:48

Fifth, the world is a vicious and brutal place. Even your friends are out to get you. They want your job, they want your house, they want your money, they want your wife, and they even want your dog. So, when people wrong you, go after those people, because it is a good feeling and because other people will see you doing it. OK? So Laura, you remember this. I always get even.

The Heligan Times

Aug. 11, 2017

A fake news trophy

President David Grump has hit out at the "fake news media" once again via Twitter for not reporting on "positive" stories. Grump tweeted that there are "so many positive things going on for Murica and the Fake News Media just doesn't want to go there."

He had also suggested that a "fake news trophy" contest should be held as to which television network covers him in the most "dishonest, corrupt and/or distorted way."

August 14th 2017

In a full and frank interview, the President laid out for the world how he sees himself.

Grump considers himself a member of "the lucky sperm club." "I mean look at me. Great genes right!"

He treats every decision he makes "like a lover," sometimes thinking with his head, other times with other parts of his body, because it reminds him to "keep in touch with my basic impulses."

And to make creative choices, he says, "I try to step back and remember my first shallow reaction. The day I realized it can be smart to be shallow was, for me, a deep experience."

He trusts no one, and places a premium on revenge. "If you don't get even, you're just a schmuck!" "I believe in an eye for an eye — like the Old Testament says."

"Some of the people who forgot to lift a finger when I needed them, when I was down, they need my help now, and I'm screwing them against the wall. I'm doing a number.... And I'm having so much fun."

Grump acknowledges he was born wealthy. "But if I had been the son of a coal miner I would have left the damn mines. But most people don't have the imagination, or whatever, to leave their mine. They just don't have it," he said.

In the past, Grump has said that he thinks he is too honest to be a politician – "too forthright."

The Heligan Times

Aug. 15, 2017

Press Secretary pressed!

The Tower Press Secretary struggled to answer questions from the press today about the President's candid interview with Prime Time News, scrambling to manage the fall-out.

2535 Rustican Road
Allegiant City
Suruina 95411

President David Grump
The Tower
Heligan City
Heligan 64617

September 4th 2017

Dear Mr President

Now it's my turn to have had a hard time.

We are back at school again – 8th Grade.

But not Ms Weber. She got let go over the summer. She wrote a piece for the local paper about bullying in schools. The Principal said she had given our school a bad name. Meanwhile, he does nothing. I will miss her.

And no Joe either. Bobby and his gang jumped him at the end of our first day. I heard that they dragged him off to the pond, tied him to a board and kept putting him under until he passed out. Trouble is that no one saw them. But the next day they were the ones going round saying, "Hey did you hear what happened to Joe Steinman? He tied himself to a board and then dunked himself in the pond 'til he passed out. Now if all the rest of the immigrants, Muslims and gays could do the same wouldn't that be great!" How are Bobby and his jerk friends allowed to stay in school after they torture someone when torture isn't legal?

I am worried that Joe is going to do something crazy. He told me he's done being the victim. I went to the Principal again, but he was too busy to see me. I heard his secretary say to him, "I've got that Laura Post outside about Joe Steinman again. Do you want to see her?" "Not particularly," I heard him reply. So rude.

The week before we went back to school, there was a gas explosion and cave in at the mine. Twenty men were trapped. Turns out the mine had not followed its own safety procedures. My dad had been warning about safety hazards for months. He and a team of other miners worked through the night to free the men. Fortunately, everyone got out alive with only minor injuries. My dad was on local TV and everyone said he was a hero. I'm so proud of him!

Part of the mine has now been closed off while an investigation takes place. My dad is worried that the owners will use their own people, so that what actually happened will be covered up. That couldn't happen could it?

And what I thought was the last straw? The tree outside my window was cut down.

Then you gave that interview on Prime Time News. OMG! Were you just not thinking? I don't know what to say. Did you want to prove that the President of Ketor was right when he insulted you?

Sincerely

Laura

PS The press is having a field day. And there is nothing fake about what they are writing, because they are simply writing direct quotes of what you said. "Too forthright" is absolutely right!

01:14

> First, I know I said "too forthright," but the way you say it makes me sound stupid. My IQ is the highest and you know it.

01:25

> Am beginning to think you are highly over rated. You cannot constantly say bad things about me. You are always complaining about me. Do you think I won't fight back? Wrong!!

01:47

> Joe won't do anything. He certainly won't fight back. He's a loser like you and will always be a victim.

The Heligan Times

Sep. 8, 2017

A storm cloud waiting to burst

Intelligence agencies have today concluded that Inferhan tried to influence the Presidential election in favor of David Grump. Evidence has been found that shows Inferhan stole information linked to rival Emily Cluster, and released it through a third party to undermine her.

Back in March then Internal Security Force Director, Alex Brush, set up an enquiry, only to be sacked by President Grump a week later over what he termed, "this Inferhan thing." In later testimony, Brush said that the President had told him, "I need loyalty, I expect loyalty and I hope you can see your way to letting this go."

In a series of tweets put out at the time, the President stated: "There is no evidence that I colluded with Inferhan. This story is FAKE NEWS and everyone knows it."

"I don't know Pooting, have no deals in Inferhan, and the haters are going crazy."

And in an apparent attempt to divert attention away from himself: "Inferhan talk is FAKE NEWS put out by the opposition, and played up by the media, in order to mask the big election defeat."

"What about all of the contacts between the Cluster campaign and Inferhan?"

Nevertheless, "this Inferhan thing" did not go away. Towards the end of March, Clarice Baker ex Internal Security Force Director was appointed as Special Counsel to investigate further. Apart from the arrest of the President's lawyer Marty Kohn in May, few details have been forthcoming of her investigation.

Grump has continued to deny any collusion with Inferhan, repeatedly calling any allegations "a witch hunt," and trying to implicate the previous administration.

At a recent press briefing, the President stated:

"If it was the GOAL of Inferhan to create discord, disruption and chaos within Murica then, with all of the committee hearings, investigations and party hatred, they have succeeded beyond their wildest dreams. They are laughing their asses off. Get smart Murica!"

"And if all of Inferhan's meddling took place during the previous administration, right up to my inauguration in January, why aren't they the subject of the investigation? Why didn't they do something about the meddling? Why aren't their crimes under investigation?"

Since March, the President's campaign manager Mark Manoerbord has been accused of accepting millions of dollars for representing the interests of Inferhan in Murica. He denied the allegations, but was formally charged with money laundering, tax and bank fraud. Mr Manoerbord has pleaded not guilty.

In May, reports surfaced of compromising material gathered by Inferhan's secret service on the President cavorting with prostitutes at a hotel in Inferhan – the so called 'golden shower tapes.' The report stated that Inferhan had "been cultivating, supporting, and assisting" David Grump for years, but had also collected damning information that was sufficient "to be able to blackmail him."

At the time, Grump dismissed claims as fake news. He tweeted: "Inferhan has never tried to use leverage over me. I HAVE NOTHING TO DO WITH INFERHAN - NO DEALS, NO LOANS, NO NOTHING!" But Prime Time News revealed that the President had been briefed by the Internal Security Force about the existence of a dossier on him.

More recently a further Grump campaign advisor admitted to making false statements to the ISF about dealings with a foreign academic, who allegedly informed him that Inferhan possessed 'dirt' on Emily Cluster.

September 9th 2017

David Grump ✅ @realDavidGrump

10:51   I never said it wasn't Inferhan who interfered. I said, "It may be Inferhan, or Ndroga or another country or group, or it may be a 400 pound genius sitting in bed and playing with his computer. The Inferhan "hoax" is that the Grump campaign colluded with Inferhan – it never did!

10:56   I strongly pressed President Pooting twice about Inferhan's meddling in our election. He vehemently denied it. I've already given my opinion.

11:03   AFTER MONTHS OF INVESTIGATIONS & COMMITTEE HEARINGS ABOUT MY "COLLUSION WITH INFERHAN," NOBODY HAS BEEN ABLE TO SHOW ANY PROOF. SAD!!

The Heligan Times

Sep. 11, 2017

Ex-Campaign manager to face new charges

Mark Manoerbord, together with ex-Inferhan spy Norit Butz, face new charges of obstruction of justice and conspiracy to obstruct justice for allegedly tampering with witnesses.

This latest indictment by Special Counsel Clarice Baker is significant beyond the charges themselves. For the first time, a senior official in David Grump's presidential campaign has been linked to Inferhan's intelligence services in a criminal matter.

If convicted, Manoerbord could face many years in prison.

September 13th 2017

David Grump ✅ @realDavidGrump

07:38   The Inferhan witch hunt hoax continues. So much time and money wasted, so many lives ruined.

07:43   This whole Inferhan Probe is Rigged. Just an excuse as to why Crooked Emily lost the Election. When will people reveal their disqualifying Conflicts of Interest?

07:54   There was No Collusion with Inferhan (except by the opposition). When will this very expensive Witch Hunt Hoax ever end? So bad for our Country. Is the Special Counsel/Justice Department leaking my lawyers' letters to the Fake News Media? Should be looking at the opposition's corruption instead?

The Heligan Times

Sep. 18, 2017

Evidence of collusion with Inferhan?

In the ever shifting world of David Grump, it is not always easy to get clarity about what he is thinking. What is clear is that he has always denied that he colluded with Inferhan. What is also clear is that he has always accused Emily Cluster and the opposition of doing so. And, he has repeatedly questioned the integrity of the previous President (something no other president has ever done), for not initiating an investigation earlier.

In addition, what has become clear over time is that through Grump's continued advocacy and support of President Pooting's agenda, the President doesn't think Inferhan did anything wrong. His actions further suggest that he does not want the full details to become known. And he seems to have no real interest in making sure Inferhan does not do the same thing again.

And that, in itself, is perhaps the most powerful evidence of collusion.

September 18th 2017

President Grump has demanded that an investigation be undertaken into whether the Internal Security Force 'infiltrated or surveilled" his campaign at the direction of the previous administration.

After what has become his daily string of messages complaining about a 'witch hunt hoax,' the President has now called into question the integrity of the Internal Security Force and Special Counsel Clarice Baker.

The Murican public is split along party lines as to whether Ms Baker's investigation is warranted or not. However, almost all believe she should be allowed to complete her task. In the meantime, the President puts out a stream of accusations, theories, half truths and lies, so that no one is sure what to believe. A source close to the President said, "Grump is a master of the tactic of flooding the zone with shit."

This latest demand of an 'investigation into the investigation' appears to be part of that strategy.

The Heligan Times

Sep. 20, 2017

Special Counsel to seek clarification as to why the President fired Internal Security Force Director, Alex Brush

Since firing his then ISF Director back in March, the President has gone on record as saying he was dissatisfied with Mr Brush's performance. The President was acting within his power if this was the reason for Mr Brush's termination. The President has also said that he fired Brush because he was investigating some of Mr Grump's associates' ties with Inferhan. If this was the case, then Grump abused his power.

In a country ruled by law, like Murica, Mr Grump has no grounds for refusing a request from the Special Counsel for an interview or the subpoena which would enforce the request.

September 21st 2017

David Grump ✅ @realDavidGrump

13:53   As has been stated by numerous legal scholars, I have the absolute right to PARDON myself, but why would I do that when I have done nothing wrong?

September 21st 2017

 A Presidential pardon?

While the President has categorically stated that he has the right to pardon himself, it is not clear whether he really does have that right. What is certain is that no President has ever pardoned himself before.

2535 Rustican Road
Allegiant City
Suruina 95411

President David Grump
The Tower
Heligan City
Heligan 64617

October 7th 2017

Dear Mr President

Tonight at dinner, Mom told us that the shelter where she volunteers is going to close. 50 people, including some families will be made homeless. And why? No more funding. It just doesn't seem fair when we see all the wealth in places like Thawle and Heligan City. And there's no way for us to get any of it for ourselves or for people who need it even more, like the people from the shelter. Mom said something needs to be done. So, she's going to run for our local council.

We also talked about you. There are no new jobs in Allegiant City. But my dad said, "I'm sure that Grump is still doing his best to fight for the working man."

Are you? Still fighting for the working man? I'm not sure. I feel so frustrated. There is so much that I have been reading over the last month. None of it is good.

Are you aware that when things get uncomfortable for you, the number of tweets you put out increases? It's like you are hiding behind social media, saying mean and rude things that you wouldn't say to people's faces. Well…. I am not so sure that you wouldn't say it to their face.

What is for sure is that nothing is ever your fault; it's always someone else's. You make denial after denial. You repeat a lot. It's like you are trying to wear people down, so they get bored with listening to your constant stream of self pitying complaints. You have said, "If it was the GOAL of Inferhan to create discord, disruption and chaos within Murica then they have succeeded beyond their wildest dreams." That's so true! But the fact that you recognize this is perhaps because you do exactly the same thing yourself. You are always spreading distrust and confusion. The Heligan Times recently suggested that during the first 9 months of your Presidency you told a public lie or falsehood nearly every day – over 250 times. Other papers think that number is conservative. Your friends at the Thawle Daily put the number at over 1000. With one breath you tell another untruth and with the next you complain about fake news. Mom would say, "Pot, kettle, black."

A few days ago, Mom and I watched a movie about a powerful woman in fashion. Nothing her assistant did was good enough. Mom said the character was probably a bit of an egomaniac and narcissist. Out of curiosity, I looked up both words.

Egomania is defined as, *"the state of considering yourself to be very important and able to do anything that you want to do."*

A **narcissist** is defined as, *"a person who is overly self involved, vain and selfish; behavior is characterized by feelings of self importance, an excessive need for admiration and a lack of empathy."*

Digging a bit deeper I found a description of **narcissistic abuse** – *"when the narcissist expects others to give up their wants and feelings in order to bolster the narcissist's own need for positive esteem."* Remember when I wrote a lot of your inaugural speech for you? You said, your ideas were better than mine. Then, another time when I disagreed with you, you wanted to threaten me with a 'fat picture.'

And **narcissistic rage** – *"the uncontrollable and unexpected anger that results from a threat to a narcissist's self esteem or worth. Rages are based on fear and will endure even after the threat has gone."* Think about your recent tweets, lashing out at a world you believe is out to get you. Or your constant battle against the press, who you see as refusing to write about "all the good things that are going on in our country." Or what you said in that ill judged interview with Prime Time News about "having so much fun" screwing people to the wall who hadn't helped you in the past.

I'm upset that this all sounds just like you. If so, then no wonder that you can't apologize. No wonder nothing is ever your fault, that you tell so many lies.

When we were talking about you at dinner, my dad said. "You have to admit that the President is not like all those other politicians. At least he doesn't lie." He didn't sound so sure though. And he's stopped smiling again. I didn't have the heart to tell him about your lies.

Sincerely

Laura

PS "Those other politicians" my dad was talking about…. maybe they aren't all bad.

07:32

So many questions. Such a curious little cat. You know what they say about curiosity and the cat right? It killed the damn cat! You know something else? I can't resist hitting you verbally when you start up, Lightweight Laura, because you are just so pathetic and easy, and by that, I mean stupid! Think of that fat photo…. FAT FACE, FAT FACE!

The Heligan Times

Oct.11, 2017

Steel and aluminum tariffs to be imposed

Plans to impose tariffs of 25% on steel and 10% on aluminum were formally announced today. "It's for the security of the country. This is the first time you'll have protection in a long while," the President told industry representatives.

His announcement to impose taxes on all steel and aluminum imports coming into Murica marks a significant move in advancing the administration's protectionist agenda. Grump acted despite objections from key advisors and pleas from car manufacturers and other heavy users of the two metals.

Only yesterday, the administration vowed that it would defend Murican industry interests against hostile powers like Inferhan and Ndroga. "Countries who engage in unfair trade practices will find that we know how to defend ourselves," said a Tower spokesperson. Today we are seeing how the President intends to defend Murican interests – through attack.

Shares in Murican metal producers were up 2-3% on the news, while the overall stock market pulled back hard as investors digested the possibility of a trade war breaking out.

October 11th 2017

David Grump ✅ @realDavidGrump

11:33   We must protect our country and our workers. Our steel industry is in bad shape. IF YOU DON'T HAVE STEEL, YOU DON'T HAVE A COUNTRY!

The Heligan Times

Oct. 12, 2017

National Economic Director resigns after failing to persuade Grump against tariffs

National Economic Director, Jeremy Stimsom, was not available for comment today, after his resignation as the President's chief economic advisor. He is just the latest in what is becoming an ever lengthening list of senior departures from the Grump administration. 7 of Grump's top 12 advisors have now left the Tower since the President's inauguration at the end of January.

October 12th 2017

Blanket tariffs have been strongly criticized by members of Grump's own party, who said the policy would cut jobs, raise prices for consumers and hit manufacturing in Murica. Trading partners have threatened retaliation in kind.

October 12th 2017

David Grump ✔ @realDavidGrump

15:21   Murica has a huge Trade Deficit because of our "very stupid" trade deals and policies. Our jobs and wealth are being given to other countries that have taken advantage of us for years. They laugh at what fools our leaders have been. No more.

15:27   To protect our Country we must protect Murican Steel and Murican steel workers! MMGA!

October 16th 2017

Back from the Brink?

This was what many trade representatives were asking as President Grump today pulled back from implementing blanket tariffs on all of Murica's trading partners. Temporary exemptions were offered to key allies and other countries with which Murica trades.

Grump then singled out Ndroga for $50bn of tariffs on a variety of goods. The President said that he would fulfill a campaign promise to close Murica's $300bn trade deficit with Ndroga. Over the past couple of days, in an attempt to stave off tariffs on its steel and aluminum exports to Murica, Ndroga had said that it would buy a further $70bn of Murican goods. This offer is now off the table.

An official from Ndroga's embassy in Heligan City vowed, "Ndroga will surely make a justified and necessary response."

The Heligan Times

Oct. 17, 2017

Trade war with Ndroga looms

A senior official from Ndroga's Foreign Ministry said, "If Murica takes unilateral and protectionist measures that harm Ndroga's interests, we will respond immediately by taking the necessary decisions to safeguard our legitimate rights and interests."

Ndroga has already drawn up a list of $50bn in Murican products that would face retaliatory tariffs, including beef and soybeans, clearly targeting Grump's rural supporters in Murica.

"If you end up with a tariff battle, you will end up with price inflation, and you could end up with consumer debt. These are all historic ingredients for an economic slowdown," former National Economic Director, Jeremy Stimson, said at an event sponsored by the Thawle Daily.

October 16th 2017

David Grump ✅ @realDavidGrump

14:31   When a country (Murica) is losing many billions of dollars on trade with virtually every country it does business with, trade wars are good, and easy to win. Example, when we are down $100 billion with a certain country and they get cute, don't trade anymore – we win big. It's easy!

15:45   Will be making a decision soon on the appointment of new National Economic Director. Many people wanting the job - will choose wisely!

October 19th 2017

David Grump ✅ @realDavidGrump

09:33   Harry Dither will be my new National Economic Director. Our Country can look forward to many years of Great Economic & Financial Success, with low taxes, unparalleled innovation, fair trade and an ever expanding labor force leading the way! MMGA

October 23rd 2017

David Grump ✅ @realDavidGrump

09:54   Our Steel and Aluminum industries (and many others) have been decimated by decades of unfair trade and bad policy with countries from around the world. We must not let our country, companies and workers be taken advantage of any longer. We want free, fair and SMART TRADE!

October 26th 2017

 Temporary exemptions from steel and aluminum tariffs given to Murica's key trading partners and allies were revoked today. Murica will now impose tariffs on steel and aluminum imports from all its key trading partners, the Grump administration said, raising the specter of a trade war with some of Heligan's closest allies.

As originally announced, the plan will place a 25% tariff on steel and a 10% tariff on aluminum imported from these countries. But unlike the recent tariffs on Ndroga's metals, these could have a significant effect on Murican consumer prices. While Ndroga accounts for 8% and 13% of steel and aluminum imports respectively, the group of economies that will now be affected together supply 50% and 60% of all steel and aluminum imported by Murica.

Reaction has been swift and reaction has been angry. All governments have said that they will impose tariffs "in kind" on Murican steel and aluminum. Some have vowed to challenge the decision in the international courts. Others are considering what they are calling at this stage, "other measures." Both Murica's neighbors issued a joint statement saying they would target several Murican exports – including steel and pipe products, berries, pork chops, and cheese – "up to an amount comparable to the level of damage" from Murican tariffs.

The Ndroga Trade Commissioner also weighed in. "This move can be compared to blackmail. President Grump will find that none of Murica's trading partners, including Ndroga, will negotiate with a gun to our heads."

Members of Grump's own party also question today's decision. "The countries singled out today are our allies. They are not Ndroga. You don't treat allies the same way as you treat opponents," said Senator John Spragg. Senator Julia Ebury called the move "dumb." "Tariffs are nearly always net negative. They benefit a select few while making everyone else worse off."

An expert in international trade, speaking at a conference on Globalization and Free Trade in Thawle said, "These measures are likely to move the globe further away from an open, fair and rules-based trade system, with adverse effects for both the Murican economy and for trading partners."

October 26th 2017

David Grump 🔵 @realDavidGrump

21:13   Our allies are wonderful countries who treat Murica very badly on trade. Now complaining about the tariffs on Steel & Aluminum. If they drop their horrific barriers & tariffs on Murican products going in, we will likewise drop ours. Big Deficit. If not, we Tax Cars etc. FAIR!

The Heligan Times

Oct. 30, 2017

Murican steel and aluminum industries – some key facts

Steel: Murica produces 10 million metric tons of steel a year. Murica imports 36 million metric tons of steel per year. The Murican steel industry has seen a huge drop in the number of people it employs from its peak of 650,000 in the 1970's, to approximately 140,000 workers today.

Aluminum: Murica produces 750,000 metric tons of aluminum per year. It imports 5 million metric tons each year. The industry employs 160,000 workers.

Overall, the steel and aluminum industries account for 0.7% of the Murican economy. The numbers of people employed in both industries equates to 0.002% of the Murican labor force.

While jobs may be added in the steel and aluminum industries, there are likely to be far higher job losses in metal intensive sectors like machinery and transport manufacture. Equally, any tariffs exacted by Murica's trading partners will increase Murica's already ballooning trade deficit.

October 31st 2017

President Grump's National Economic Director, Harry Dither, was admitted to hospital today. He was said to be suffering from heart arrhythmia and stress. Mr Dither has been in office for just 12 days.

October 31st 2017

David Grump ✅ @realDavidGrump

11:39   Our Great Harry Dither, who has been working so hard on trade and the economy, has just suffered a heart attack. Get well soon Harry!

15:43   Tariffs are the greatest! Either a country which has treated Murica unfairly on Trade negotiates a fair deal or it gets hit with tariffs.   It's as simple as that – and everybody's talking! Remember, we are the 'piggy bank' that's being robbed. All will be Great!

2535 Rustican Road
Allegiant City
Suruina 95411

President David Grump
The Tower
Heligan City
Heligan 64617

November 5th 2017

Dear Mr President

Today I heard my dad's mine is to close. They say that it's "no longer economic to operate."

My dad's boss told him that the investigation into mine safety after the explosion and collapse a few months back had been completed. The final report called for a lot of modernization of the mine and much of its machinery – in particular its elevators and shaft and roof support systems. All of this uses steel, which the mine owners anticipate will now be going up in price. In addition, nearly all the coking coal from my dad's mine is exported to Ndroga. They say that because of your tariffs and the push back that is happening as a result, the markets for my dad's coal are "unlikely to remain economic." "We just have to be cautious until we know more details."

The day the announcement was made two men were so depressed that they shot themselves. My dad's last day is next Friday. He is hoping to be hired as one of the skeleton crew that will look after the closed mine. But so is everyone else.

I am not an economist, although I want to be, but even I know that if you start slapping taxes and tariffs on a bunch of goods, you will be raising the prices on the Murican consumer. You will also be hurting the people who voted for you. What were you thinking? Or did you just not think this through?

Knowing you, you will say that these tariffs are a negotiating tactic to get trade terms that are fair. However, what you are doing is very risky. High risk is no doubt a positive factor for you, as you believe that you can do anything and beat anybody. But it's one thing to take risks with your own money, quite another when it's other peoples' jobs and lives that are at stake. The forgotten men and women in Allegiant City are hurting badly. They feel forgotten again. During your campaign you promised that their needs would be addressed. At your inaugural speech you made them another promise that "every decision on trade, on taxes, on immigration, on foreign affairs will be made to benefit Murican workers and Murican families." We haven't seen many benefits. With the closing of my dad's mine, things have actually gotten worse.

It feels like your tariffs are the same as Sam and Bobby fighting or you and Yun Kwang when you said, "I too have a Nuclear Button, but it is much bigger and more powerful than his, and my button works!" So, when Ndroga comes back with tariffs of their own, I'm guessing you will increase your tariffs to $200bn or $300bn. Really? Anything you can do I can do bigger and better?

Sincerely

Laura

PS If you continue, then many more people who supported you will end up hurting. You will lose their support. Is that what you want?

You say, "Tariffs are the greatest," and "Trade wars are good and easy to win." My new Social Studies teacher says, "History shows that no one wins a trade war."

The Heligan Times

Nov. 9, 2017

One year on - a mixed economic review?

The Murican economy continues to grow.

Corporate profits beat expectations during the year, unemployment has dropped to 4.1% and share prices have continued to climb. However, a year after President Grump was elected, the factories have not roared back. Tax cuts, which were heralded by the President as leading to more jobs for Murican workers, have in practice led to a few companies paying bonuses, an increase in share by back schemes benefiting those companies' shareholders, and companies hoarding cash for an expected downturn in the economy. There is no evidence that companies have re-invested in more workers.

Although Murican stock markets have continued to climb, much of this is fueled by companies that have more than half of their revenue coming from overseas. Energy, materials and technology companies have all shown double digit growth this year. In contrast, consumer staples and discretionary stocks along with utilities, industrials and telecommunications have only increased by 2.4%. And the threat of a trade war has seen a recent pullback.

Thursday, November 9, 2017

10:24

> You're certainly right about not being an economist. As if! Loser. You are also right about tariff's being a negotiating tactic. You're wrong about everything else. Sad!

10:34

> You don't understand how to do a deal. Nobody can beat me on doing deals. I am the best dealmaker. You're a stupid baby, a lightweight. Poor little Lightweight Laura. Although you are not so little are you – FAT FACE!

November 13th 2017

This just in.

We are getting reports that a gunman using a semi-automatic rifle killed 10 people and injured 12 others at Annabel Bishop School in Allegiant City today.

This is the latest in what has become an epidemic of school shootings.

November 15th 2017

David Grump ✅ @realDavidGrump

21:14   My prayers and condolences to the families of the victims of the terrible Suruina shooting. No child, teacher or anyone else should ever feel unsafe in a Murican school.

The Heligan Times

Nov.15, 2017

Words of comfort, but no policy change after Annabel Bishop School shooting

Two days after the deadly school shooting in Allegiant City by Joe Steinman, the President offered words of comfort but no policy changes to a grieving nation.

"To every parent, teacher, and child who is hurting so badly, we are here for you, whatever you need, whatever we can do, to ease your pain. We are all joined together as one Murican family, and your suffering is our burden also."

He went on to say, "It is not enough to take actions that make us feel like we are making a difference. We must actually make that difference."

November 15th 2017

David Grump ✅ @realDavidGrump

12:19   So many signs that the Suruina shooter was mentally disturbed, even expelled from school for bad and erratic behavior. Neighbors and classmates knew he was a big problem. Must always report such instances to authorities, again and again!

November 15th 2017

Grump calls the response of the police to the Annabel Bishop School shooting "disgusting." "I would have run in, even if I didn't have a weapon," he told reporters.

The Heligan Times

Nov. 18, 2017

To arm or not to arm

In a series of tweets, the President tried to set the record straight about arming teachers:

"I never said "give teachers guns" like was stated on Fake Prime Time News. What I said was to look at the possibility of giving concealed guns to gun adept teachers with military or special training experience – only the best. 20% of teachers, a lot, would now be able to immediately fire back if a savage sicko came to a school with bad intentions. Highly trained teachers would also serve as a deterrent to the cowards that do this. Far more assets at much less cost than guards. A "gun free" school is a magnet for bad people. ATTACKS WOULD END!"

President David Grump
The Tower
Heligan City
Heligan 64617

December 3rd 2017

Dear Mr President

Let me set the record straight.

When the fire alarm went off at school on November 13th, everyone thought it was just a drill. It wasn't. Joe had pulled the alarm so that Bobby and his gang would come running out. The newspapers are all saying he was mentally unstable, that mental instability is the reason why we have so many gun related crimes. But Joe was not mentally unstable. He had been bullied and abused by Bobby and his gang since kindergarten. Every day. For 7 long years.

No adult had ever stood up to protect him. Like you said, I reported what was going on to the 'authorities again and again.' And the best the Principal could do was send Joe home to keep him safe. But Joe was not the problem. Bobby was. And no action was taken against Bobby.

Yesterday, Joe came to school late, as he always did. The only difference was that he was wearing a Grump Halloween mask and carrying an AR-15 semi-automatic rifle – one of 10 guns that his dad owned. Things went crazy, fast. As kids ran out of their classrooms, Joe was waiting. He found Bobby and his four friends, shot and killed them. People started screaming. They were struggling to get away from the shooting, trampling over each other. Some were caught in the crossfire including our teacher Ms Ironside. Joe then locked himself into the boy's bathroom. I persuaded him to let me in to talk. He was crying. A while back, he'd somehow gotten hold of my phone again, but this time he'd seen your text about him. You know the one that said, 'Joe won't do anything. He certainly won't fight back. He's a loser like you and will always be a victim.'

"Well I guess I showed Grump," he said.

Then, through his tears, Joe said to me, "You are my only friend. Don't let them say I was crazy. You know what I've been through. Bobby didn't deserve to live."

He wouldn't give me his gun. I tried inching closer to him. "I'll be locked away forever," he said. "Laura, make sure my life counts for something. Make my death count." I grabbed for him, but he was too quick and he shot himself. All I could do was hold him as he died in my arms. He literally died in my arms! It was the worst day of my life.

I still hear the gunshots. I hear the screams. I see people running and falling. I see the pools of blood. I can't get the sounds and the images out of my head. But mostly I can't get Joe out of my head and the fact that he'd seen your text.

When I close my eyes to go to sleep it's worse.

This could have been avoided with better teaching, better protection and better gun laws. Murica failed both Joe and Bobby. You failed them. And I failed them.

Why can't we solve this problem which exists nowhere else in the world? Other countries with tighter gun controls have fewer mass shootings, murders, and cases of domestic violence in which guns are involved. They do not have our problem. I'm still only 13. If I can see the connection, why can't you?

All I had to do was google 'mass shootings' to find out just how deadly our problem is. Did you know that in the last five years, Murica has had over 1600 mass shootings costing 1836 lives? This is more than 3 times the number of Murican military deaths over the same period. And how many of these have been school shootings? Over 300 – more than one per week. It's all right there on the internet.

I have learned in Social Studies class that the gun laws we have were based on the right to bear arms. They were drawn up nearly 250 years ago, when we were fighting to get free from colonial powers. Times have changed; guns have changed and become so much more powerful and dangerous. Our gun laws have not. We have changed other laws. Why can't we change our laws about guns which bring so much death and destruction?

I read what you said about it not being enough to do things that make us feel we are making a difference, "we must actually make that difference." You are right. So, what are you doing? Arming teachers? Seriously? Who wants their 1st Grade teacher to be carrying a gun? What sort of message does that send to kids growing up? A couple of my teachers, Ms Cynthia and Ms Marion are so lame that they would end up shooting themselves by mistake. If I wasn't so angry I'd laugh. I wish you were "only joking" about this. Arming teachers is one of the dumbest ideas I have ever heard.

So, Mr President, I make a solemn promise to you. You keep on tweeting, but like Mom, I will act to make a difference. I will be the change I want to see.

Sincerely

Laura Post

PS Guess what I found when I looked up the Murican Gun Association? I found out that a few months ago, you signed a bill repealing a law that had made it harder for people with mental illnesses to purchase a gun. Is that what you call making a difference?

00:05

> Stand down. I can see the blood coming out of your eyes. The blood coming out of your wherever. You must have been born stupid. I am certainly not stupid. You don't know how government works. Tougher gun laws do not decrease violence. Good guys with guns stop bad guys with guns. That's the way it's always been in Murica. You're a stupid girl, a lightweight, so pathetic.

00:34

> It was a huge mistake to mess with me. Remember, you started this. If I can rain down fire and fury on Ketor and that dumb, dopey clown Yun Kwang, imagine how easy it will be for me to make you 'disappear.' Then you won't just be a stupid fat girl. You'll be a stupid gone girl.

December 8th 2017

Prime Time News
PTN.COM

Laura Post to David Grump – "Our generation."

In a moving speech to parents, students and press outside the Annabel Bishop School, 13 year old Laura Post, classmate of Joe Steinman, challenged the President to change the gun laws of Murica.

"I was born in 2003. Mass shootings and gun violence have been a tragic backdrop to my life. I know they have been to yours too. Thank you for standing here with me today."

"If all our government and President can do is send thoughts and prayers, then it's time for us – who are also the victims of gun violence – to be the change that we want to see."

"Today we should be home grieving. But today I ask you to join me. Today I ask you to fight, not just for the tragic victims of the shooting here at Annabel Bishop School, but for all the victims of gun violence in Murica."

"We must fight against domestic violence made deadly by guns. We must fight to make suicide harder for kids and adults suffering from mental illness. We must fight to make our streets safe so that innocent children don't get caught in the crossfire of gang violence. We must fight to make people realize that this is an issue that affects all of us."

"In Suruina, you don't need a permit to buy a gun; you don't need a gun license. In fact, you can buy as many guns as you want at one time. Hallelujah! And, once you buy your guns, you don't even need to register them. Then you just go ahead and carry your concealed rifles and shotguns, because you don't need a permit for that either."

"Adults may have gotten used to saying, "Things are what they are." But with guns, if you do nothing, people will keep on ending up dead. So, it's time we start to do something."

"I hear a lot of yammer about our generation being entitled and needy. But who is the generation that will fight so that all lives matter as much as the millions of dollars politicians get each election from the Murican Gun Association? Our generation!"

"Who is the generation that will fight so that we are safe in our homes, in our malls and movie theatres? Our generation!"

"Who is the generation that will fight to ensure our teachers are armed with resources not guns? Our generation!"

"We are the largest, most educated, most diverse generation there has ever been. We are the generation that will end gun violence in Murica."

Her moving speech was broadcast around the world.

Later, plans were announced for nationwide protests to take place on January 20th with a March Against Guns in the nation's capital.

The Heligan Times

Dec. 8, 2017

Gun poll latest

A new poll suggests that 67% of Muricans back a nationwide ban on assault rifles.

08:32

> You need to stop writing to me.

December 24th 2017

David Grump ✅ @realDavidGrump

17:35   People are proud to be saying Merry Christmas again. I am proud to have led the charge against the assault of our cherished and beautiful phrase. MERRY CHRISTMAS!!!!!

17:40   Merry Christmas to all!

17:43   MERRY CHRISTMAS!!

2535 Rustican Road
Allegiant City
Suruina 95411

President David Grump
The Tower
Heligan City
Heligan 64617

January 12th 2018

Dear Mr President

My birthday's passed. So has Christmas. And the New Year. In a few days we will
march.

Since the shooting, there has been too much time to think and too much time to
feel. I have been so confused and so angry. At school, we have been given a lot
of freedom in what we study. I have found escape and comfort in myths and folk
tales and in particular the stories of Hans Christian Andersen. There is one in
particular that I like....

————————

Many years ago, there was an Emperor, who was exceedingly fond of new
clothes. You probably know the story. But please read it again. It's important.

Remember? Two swindlers come to the great city where the Emperor lives. They
let it be known they are weavers, who can weave the most magnificent fabrics
imaginable. Not only are their colors and patterns uncommonly fine, but clothes
made of this cloth have a wonderful way of becoming invisible to anyone who is
unfit for his office, or who is unusually stupid.

"Those would be just the clothes for me," thinks the Emperor. "If I wear them I
will be able to discover which men in my empire are unfit for their posts. And I
can tell the wise men from the fools." He pays the two swindlers a large sum of
money to start work at once.

They set up two looms and pretend to weave, though there is NOTHING on the looms. All the finest silk and the purest gold thread which they demand goes straight into their traveling bags, while they work the empty looms far into the night.

After a while, the Emperor wants to know how the weavers are getting on, but he remembers that those who are unfit for their position will not be able to see the fabric, so he sends a trusted minister in his place.

The poor minister, of course, cannot see any cloth on the looms. Fearing that he may be thought a fool or unfit for office, he tells the Emperor, "It's beautiful; it's enchanting."

Soon, the whole town is talking of the splendid cloth. Having 'seen' his new clothes for himself, the Emperor is persuaded to wear them at a great procession he is soon to lead.

The day of the procession arrives and the Emperor is dressed in the clothes made from the wonderful fabric.

Everyone watching in the streets says, "Oh, how fine are the Emperor's new clothes! Don't they fit him to perfection? And see his long train!" Nobody will say they can't see anything, for that would prove them either unfit for their position, or a fool.

Until a little child says, "But he hasn't got anything on."

Then, one person whispers to another what the child has said, "He hasn't anything on. A child says he hasn't anything on."

"But he hasn't got anything on!" the whole town cries out at last.

The Emperor shivers, for he suspects they are right. But he thinks, "This procession has got to go on." So, he walks more proudly than ever, as his noblemen hold high the train that isn't there at all.

Mr President, in this story, it seems to me that you are BOTH the Emperor and the swindlers who cheated him.

You are the Emperor obsessed, not with clothes, but with yourself. So much of what you say is about you and how you are the smartest and the best. No one can do what you do, because everyone else is an incompetent, stupid loser. The other side to your boasting is putting down anyone who disagrees with you and blaming others for anything that goes wrong. Like the emperor's courtiers, the people that surround you know that if they say anything that is against what you believe, they will be ridiculed as unfit for office and fools and then fired. If they want to stay in their position, they have to lie to themselves and be blind to the truth.

You are also a swindler. It feels like you cheat yourself. You appear to be completely lacking in self awareness – no one is as wonderful as you believe yourself to be. While you can control the people around you with fear, ridicule and threatening loss of power, you cannot do that with the media. So, you detest the reporters and the news outlets, that refuse to kiss up to you and give you the recognition that you believe you deserve. And yet I know the media eat away at you, causing you to doubt yourself just as the Emperor did.

It feels like you have also swindled and cheated the people of Murica. You promised to keep working for us, to fight for us and help turn things around, to Make Murica Great Again, to never let us down. But you have let us down – again and again. Every time you have chosen to focus on yourself rather than the needs of your voters, you have shown your ugly empty side. And through your behavior, you have destroyed the respect that is due to the office of the President. Like the people in the story, the people of Murica will end up no longer respecting you.

Why? Because I am the child who says out loud what so many people are thinking yet too afraid to say, "But he hasn't got anything on." Mr President, you are wearing no clothes. Are you starting to shiver yet?

I see through you, because I understand you.

And I hate that I pity you.

Sincerely

Laura Post

PS I have a feeling that you will get your wish for me to stop writing to you soon enough.

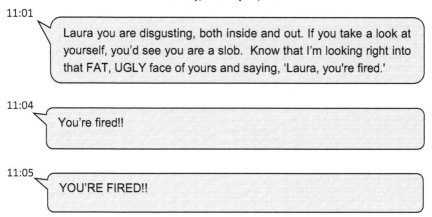

11:01

Laura you are disgusting, both inside and out. If you take a look at yourself, you'd see you are a slob. Know that I'm looking right into that FAT, UGLY face of yours and saying, 'Laura, you're fired.'

11:04

You're fired!!

11:05

YOU'RE FIRED!!

The Heligan Times

Jan. 20, 2018

Laura Post is slain by Heligan sniper

In front of an audience in excess of 500,000 marchers, 14 year old Laura Post took to the stage which marked the end of her March Against Guns rally in the nation's capital. Similar marches have taken place in major cities across Murica.

This time a year ago, David Grump was sworn in as President.

"Seven minutes and about fifteen seconds," she said. "In a little over 7 minutes, 10 of our classmates and friends were taken from us, 12 more were injured and everyone in our community was forever changed. Anyone who was there understands. Anyone who has been touched by the horror of gun violence understands."

Wiping away tears, she repeated the names of each of the victims and the things they would never do again. Then, as a sign of respect, she stopped speaking.

Silence gripped Post and her audience for several minutes. Her head bowed, Post stood immobile until two shots rang out. Amidst chaos and screams, Post fell to the ground.

She was rushed to Heligan's Central Hospital, but was pronounced dead on arrival.

2535 Rustican Road
Allegiant City
Suruina 95411

President David Grump
The Tower
Heligan City
Heligan 64617

January 20th 2018

Dear Mr President

Surprise!

You were probably hoping not to hear from me again or perhaps you were sure that you wouldn't! I have hoped for many things over the past two years I have been writing to you, but as far as you are concerned, I have learned that hope is not a plan. So, here is my plan.

I am scared, so scared. Scared about what I have started. Scared about whether I can deliver change. Scared about the march today and how exposed I will be.

For the past few days there has been a black SUV parked down the road from our house. I walked up to it on my way to school yesterday but it drove away. Then it was back again in the afternoon. I know you could 'disappear' me, as you say, make me a gone girl. Though it's not just you who doesn't like what I am saying. There are people out there who would see it as poetic justice if I got shot.

But even though I am scared, I am more determined to act. So, the first part of my plan is to march.

In the days since the school shooting, I said that there had been a lot of time to think and feel. I have done a lot of both.

Two years ago, when I first started writing these letters, I was happy and excited. Happy that you were going to help my dad and people like him. Excited just to be writing to you. Then, as time went by, there was confusion and a feeling of being let down, an awful sense that I had been wrong about you. And now?

Now, I realize I am not angry, I'm frustrated. Frustrated in the knowledge that Mom and my dad, and so many others like them, have struggled their whole adult lives to create opportunity and a better life for their children and have failed. They remain forgotten. The Murican Dream is dead.

I am not angry, I am sad – really sad. I am sad because of the hypocrisy of religious leaders who support you and turn not just one, but two blind eyes to your horrible behavior; I am sad that our country is more divided than ever; I am sad because of the sheer hopelessness that so many people in Murica now feel.

I am not angry, I am ashamed. Ashamed of you Mr President. You promised so much and have delivered so little; you believe you have the right to harass, grope and f**k any woman you choose and then boast about it; you call women you don't like, fat pigs, dogs, ugly slobs, disgusting animals; you are so caught up in yourself that everything has to be about you; you ignore global warming; you ignore LGBTQ issues; you have set back the clock on a woman's right to choose; you lie. The list goes on and on. Worst of all Mr President, you are a bully and a racist – even if you haven't incited hate speech, a lot of what you say about immigrants and foreigners is hateful. You have developed a taste for discrimination where the benefits outweigh the costs for you. So you will continue to be like this unless you are called out.

Mr President, you called out Crooked Emily. Well now I am calling you out.

What are you afraid of? What are you covering up with your bragging, your act of being smart, your desperate need for attention and recognition? What will it say about you and your Presidency if two of your top aides, Marty Kohn and Mark Manoerbord, are found guilty? What will prosecutors find when Melody Melons testifies? What will the Special Counsel uncover with regards to your campaign's relationship with Inferhan? What would the Government Revenue Service find if they looked at the tax returns that you refused to disclose?

Mr President, you no longer have my trust.

You no longer have my support.

You no longer have my 'vote.'

I guess you can take some satisfaction however. Because if you are reading this, I am dead. I have 'disappeared.'

So, what was the second part of my plan? The second part was to make Mom promise that she'd post this letter after the march today if anything happened to me. Mom was reluctant to let me go, but she realized that however small I may be physically, this was a fight I couldn't walk away from. And she agrees with me.

I am glad I went down fighting. And not fighting you, but fighting for something I believed in. At the end of the day, that is what will bring about change. Your opposition and others who want positive change have to stop fighting amongst themselves. They have to stop simply being against you and say what they are for. That is what I have tried to model.

The third part? My dad made me a promise too. He promised to forward copies of our correspondence to the Heligan Times and Prime Time News if I didn't come home – if I was disappeared.

You see, while he's not totally convinced by my arguments about you, he understands and respects my point of view – something you do not.

He is a true hero. He has never let me down.

Sincerely

Laura Post

PS I have tried to forgive you and can't find it in my heart to do it. You have killed me Mr President, both emotionally and physically.

January 24th 2018

The nation mourns as Laura Post is buried.

Laura Post was laid to rest today. In a quiet ceremony at the local church where she worshipped each Sunday, family and friends gathered to pay their last respects. The world's press was also in attendance. Laura caught the world's imagination with her moving speech and subsequent interviews following the tragic shooting at the Annabel Bishop School in Allegiant City last month.

Laura was fatally shot by an assassin on January 20th as she spoke to a crowd of what is now thought to be 800,000 people at the March Against Guns rally in Heligan. This is more than double the number of supporters who were present at President Grump's inauguration speech a year ago.

No trace has been found of the sniper except a stray bullet casing of the type only used by Murican Special Forces. The casing was found on a rooftop 400 yards from where Laura was standing.

The Heligan Times

Jan. 26, 2018

Laura Post's letters published

Laura Post's extraordinary correspondence with President Grump was published today.

Readers have been blown away. The overwhelming emotions seem to be ones of shame, amazement and respect – shame that people have simply been spectators of the Grump Presidency; amazement and respect for the young girl who engaged so powerfully with David Grump.

She has been named Murican Magazine's Person of the Year for organizing the March Against Guns rally earlier this month, for calling the President out for his unbecoming behavior and "wearing no clothes." Murican Magazine calls her one of the great Silence Breakers.

January 29th2018

Special Counsel, Clarice Baker, has subpoenaed President Grump's tax returns for the last 10 years as part of her investigation into Inferhan's interference with the Murican election in 2016. Because the President refused to publish his tax returns, it has never been possible to identify what foreign business ventures are included in his filings and what this says about where Mr Grump has financial interests. In particular, the people of Murica have never known whether the President had any ties to Inferhan prior to becoming President. They have only had his denials.

January 30th 2018

Miners march on Heligan City

In the largest march in the nation's history, members of the Miners' Union, the Steel & Metal Workers' Union, the Transport & General Workers' Union, the Teachers' Union and many others came together in our capital to present a petition to the Senate signed by 15 million people. The petition demands that wide ranging gun control legislation be enacted at a national level.

Union members were joined by every cross section of society – different ethnic and immigrant groups, Jewish, Muslim, and Christian groups, huge numbers from the LGBTQ community, children with their parents, members from different branches of the military, farm workers, environmentalists.

People from Grump's base mixed with lesbian and gay groups. Representatives of all political colors walked side by side.

Police and security personnel kept a respectful distance from what was a peaceful but somehow celebratory occasion. Seeing so many groups merge together around a common purpose in which all could find meaning was extremely powerful.

John Post, the father of Laura Post, wearing his miner's overalls, addressed the crowds from the steps of the Senate.

"Thank you. Thank you all. My family owes you a huge debt of gratitude for the outpouring of love we have received since Laura's untimely death ten days ago. And I know that Laura would want me to thank you for taking forward the movement she started to enact national gun control legislation."

"I have learned from her that we can always work to make things better. On the day of the march, she was determined to do just that – make things better for Murica. She was upbeat, saying she felt positive that others would too. You see she died with hope in her heart."

Visibly moved, the crowd remained completely silent. "By coming here today, you have given voice to Laura's hope and have all absolutely made things better. Thank you."

There was a pause, as Laura's father tried to control his own emotions. He looked out over the sea of people and continued:

"I was sitting in Laura's room last night and I found something she was writing. It turns out it was a last letter. A letter that she wrote to you, the Murican people. I'd like to read it to you."

"It is dated January 20th 2018, the same date as her last letter to President Grump. The date of her death."

"Dear Murica, Listen up. It's time!"

"We the People of Murica, in order to form a more perfect Union, establish Justice, insure domestic Tranquility, provide for the common defense, promote the general Welfare, and secure the Blessings of Liberty to ourselves and those who come after us, do ordain and establish our Constitution."

"When I read these words, I am inspired. But when I read more closely, I start to question."

"Are we a perfect Union when such a small percentage of our population controls such a high percentage of our nation's wealth?"

"Have we established justice, when migrant children are forced to be separated from their parents and put in cages?"

144

"Can we say there is domestic tranquility when rates of domestic violence are through the roof?"

"As a child or young adult, is it safe to go out in every part of our inner cities?"

"Are we doing enough to promote general welfare when healthcare is not available to all who need it?"

"Are we truly secure in the blessings of liberty when levels of household debt are now the highest they have ever been?"

"So, what does that leave? It leaves, "We the people." There is power in 'We.' Murica, we have significant problems. Murica, we are not easy. But I believe that if we listen to each other and use the 'Power of We,' we will realize that we are so much more than the sum of our parts. Then we will be able to put out the flames of mistrust and hate that divide us and start to solve our problems. It's time!"

"One problem we can solve is our leadership. It's time!"

"It's time we recognized that our President believes in the 'Power of I.'"

"We have learned not to trust politicians who have done too little for too long to make our lives better. They have given us endless promises but done nothing. David Grump was different. He shone a light on those broken promises. He made us feel listened to. He set himself up as our strong man and our protector."

"Then he went on to feed our fears and identified different groups to blame for our situation – Muslims and immigrants, who he said were trying to take our jobs and push crime rates ever higher. And we voted for him in huge numbers."

"Finally, he questioned the institutions that we trust – the free press, the Internal Security Force, the independent investigation of the Special Counsel. He has misinformed us and lied to us to undermine their credibility. As a result, he has undermined our democracy. And he has done this in our name."

"With the President, there is a cost to speaking out. We cannot wait for that cost to become too high. We cannot wait for him to start locking people up who disagree with him."

"Mr President, you have not treated the Murican people with respect. Nevertheless, it is with respect that we the people ask you to step down. It's time!"

"Her letter ended there. She signed it and drew a picture of a rainbow – a burst of color after a storm, symbolizing hope, peace and a brighter future."

John Post paused while the crowd cheered and applauded his daughter. He looked out across the huge crowd again and took a deep breath. Then, with tears in his eyes and his voice breaking, he went on:

"Laura, as your father, I always knew you were special. Yet it is only in the last few weeks that I have learned quite how extraordinary you were. Although you have disappeared from this world at far too young an age, your influence will live on. We will love you forever."

"You and your generation will make the world a better place. But, 'we the people' cannot expect you, our children, to fix all the problems that we have created. As a husband, father, brother and son, I ask all generations to come together so that we fulfil Laura's dream of making a better Murica and truly do secure the blessings of liberty to ourselves and those who come after us."

He closed with his daughter's rallying call, "It's time!"

The crowd then took up the call in a deafening chant, "It's time! It's time!"

The message to the President Grump is clear.

The Heligan Times

Feb. 7, 2018

President to be impeached

An impeachment process against David Grump was formally initiated today, when the Senate's Judiciary Committee was given authority to investigate whether sufficient grounds existed to impeach David Grump, 45th President of Murica, of high crimes and misdemeanors, primarily related to Inferhan's interference with the 2016 election.

The Heligan Times

Jun. 4, 2018

Articles of impeachment approved

The Senate's Judiciary Committee today approved four articles of impeachment against Grump – obstruction of justice, abuse of power, contempt of the Senate and unbecoming conduct.

June 14th 2018

Grump resigns!

With his political support completely eroded, Grump resigned from office today. Had he not resigned, his impeachment and removal from office by a trial before the Murican Senate was set to have taken place on July 2nd.

The Heligan Times

Jul. 4, 2018

Ex-President Grump arrested on charges of tax evasion

David Grump was escorted from his home in handcuffs today by officers of the Internal Security Force. A trial date has been set for later this month.

The Heligan Times

Ex-President Grump convicted of tax evasion

David Grump was today sentenced to 11 years in prison for not paying taxes in 2013 and 2014. He also faces a tax bill in the hundreds of millions of dollars plus interest.

Government investigators were first tipped off about Grump's tax returns by comments in the correspondence between the ex-President and Laura Post. Early in their correspondence Ms Post wrote to the then Presidential candidate, "Please tell me you did nothing illegal with your taxes?" A few days later Grump texted back, "Trust me, whether I did anything illegal or not, the Murican people will forget about my tax returns soon enough," never denying that he had acted illegally.

It was Ms Post's correspondence which led to the initial subpoena of Grump's tax returns and the subsequent initiation of impeachment proceedings.

January 20th 2019

Twelve months to the day, the gunman who shot and killed Laura Post remains at large.

Acknowledgements

This book could not have been written without the input, love and support of Bella.

We would like to thank print and television journalists everywhere, who focus on delivering factual and balanced news content and coverage.

Special thanks to the Hans Christian Andersen Center at SDU in Denmark, for permission to print parts of the story of the Emperor's New Clothes used by Laura in one of her letters. This is from a translation by actor Jean Hersholt, (1886-1956).

Finally, we would like to thank Josh, Ellie, Betsy, Tony, Katrina and Chris for their feedback and encouragement in shaping the book and getting Laura's letters published.

John Post
Allegiant City   March 2019

Printed in Great Britain
by Amazon